Wrapped in a Riddle

Sharon E. Heisel

Houghton Mifflin Company
Boston 1993

Library of Congress Cataloging-in-Publication Data

Heisel, Sharon E.
  Wrapped in a riddle / by Sharon E. Heisel.
    p. cm.
  Summary: While staying at the Jumping Frog Inn, a bed-and-
breakfast establishment run by her grandmother, eleven-year-old
Miranda investigates a mystery involving stolen letters supposedly
written by Mark Twain.
  ISBN 0-395-65026-7
  [1. Mystery and detective stories.]   I. Title.
PZ7.H3688Wr 1993   92-26954
[Fic] — dc20   CIP
                          AC

Printed in the United States of America

AGM 10 9 8 7 6 5 4 3 2 1

This book is for my best friend, Manville.

Chapter 1

"What is the end of everything?"

My grandmother's note lay on the kitchen table, anchored by a blue bowl filled with bright red apples. A pencil lay beside it.

The rest of the note made more sense, if you know my grandmother.

> Miranda, dear,
>
> Spring blossoms call. I'm off to soak up daffodils and sunshine. Do not despair. We shall have quiche for dinner with an amusing apple cider to drink. Have a snack. I'll be back around six.
>
> Love you,
GrandAnn
>
> P.S. What is the end of everything?

I couldn't help smiling. GrandAnn gets as excited as a child. She loves puzzles and riddles and games of all kinds. She plays at everything she does, even things most people would call work.

She even looks like a toy. She is doll-like, tiny and delicate and always cheerful. Her eyes are a lively

1

shade of blue, a color like the bright glass eyes of a porcelain doll. I could imagine her out on this sunny afternoon. She would be perching on her ruffled pillow, peering over the steering wheel, and guiding her little sports car among the fragrant hills of southern Oregon.

I hardly needed to think about the answer to her riddle. Picking up the pencil, I wrote, "The letter *g*."

I chose the reddest apple and polished it on my sleeve, then took a bite. GrandAnn wouldn't be back for at least an hour. I pushed through the swinging door out of the kitchen. It squeaked a mild protest as it swung shut behind me. I chose a book from the bookcase, then, toe to heel, I scuffed my shoes off and sank into the overstuffed sofa in the Becky Thatcher Room.

I know most houses have rooms with practical names, like bedroom and living room. My grandmother doesn't do things the practical way.

GrandAnn owns and runs a bed-and-breakfast inn called The Jumping Frog. The Jumping Frog has been in our family since it was built a century ago. GrandAnn inherited it from her grandmother, who moved here when she was twelve and the house was new. The Jumping Frog has always been an inn.

A hundred years ago, Ashville was still a gold rush town. Only a few people actually panned or dug for the precious gold. Most made their livings by providing the miners with supplies or with a warm bed and bath. Nowadays the town of Ashville depends

2

on tourists who come to see plays at The Bard's Theater or to attend the summer music festival. They don't work the mines, but they still appreciate a warm bed and bath.

GrandAnn loves to have interesting people around, so operating the inn suits her. It is more like fun than work — especially the naming of the rooms.

Each room in a bed-and-breakfast inn is supposed to have a name and a personality. When GrandAnn took over The Jumping Frog, she chose the names of characters in her favorite books by Mark Twain. The living room is named for Tom Sawyer's girlfriend, Becky Thatcher. The four guest rooms upstairs are named Tom Sawyer (of course), Huckleberry Finn (Huck for short), Pudd'nhead Wilson, and The Connecticut Yankee.

The Becky Thatcher Room has lots of personality. The sofa is covered in a bright print, with lilacs and Queen Anne's lace splashed extravagantly across the arms and back. The overstuffed chair is deep and cozy. A bookshelf under the window is well stocked with books, all by Mark Twain. The curtains are lace, and the lamps have cut glass bobbles that catch the light and throw it into the corners. It is just the sort of room a young girl like Becky would love. *I* love it.

The only somber thing in the room is a stern portrait of Samuel Clemens over the fireplace. At least he usually looks stern. Sometimes the light from the lamps' prisms will dance across his face, and I am positive his eyes twinkle. It could be just my imagination.

Samuel Clemens is one of GrandAnn's riddles. The name most people know him by is Mark Twain.

GrandAnn searches garage sales for copies of Mark Twain's books. She brings them home and puts them in the bookcase. Any guest who wants one is welcome to take it. GrandAnn believes in encouraging people to read.

The book I had picked was *Tom Sawyer*. I've read it before, but sometimes I like to reread my favorite parts. The book starts with Aunt Polly searching for Tom. She calls his name, but gets no answer. Irritated, she pokes under the bed with her broom, hoping to drive Tom out of hiding. An equally irritated cat scrambles out.

"Meow!"

I wasn't really surprised to look up and find GrandAnn's cat, Orenthal, posed in the doorway. His timing is always excellent. He repeated himself impatiently, using his "feed me" voice.

"Meow!"

Orenthal doesn't know how to say please, or at least he doesn't bother to when he is talking to me. He simply demands. It works. He stared at me expectantly and worked his paws against the carpet.

"Meow!"

I sighed, put down the book, and swung my feet off the couch. Orenthal led the way back to the kitchen, his crooked stump of a tail upright and quivering. I followed obediently.

The kitchen door squealed again as I swung it open. Then, like an echo, I heard an urgent shriek from the upstairs hall.

"No! Oh, no! Get away!"

A short silence followed, then a crash.

"Scoundrel! Traitor! Knave!"

Another crash, like cymbals clanging.

Undisturbed, I opened the can of cat food under Orenthal's serious gaze, then put his filled dish on the floor. He rewarded me with a musical purr of joy and ate enthusiastically.

"Begone, depart, away!" The voice cascaded down the stairwell, followed by another shriek.

I walked to the foot of the back stairs and called, "Hello, Mrs. Prescott. I'm home."

Mrs. Prescott's face appeared over the banister. A welcoming smile washed over her features.

"Hi, Miranda. I was just rehearsing. Hope I didn't bother you."

She gestured with a dustpan in one hand and a broom in the other. Another cymbal-like crash echoed down the stairwell.

"No bother. How's the melodrama coming?"

Mrs. Prescott and GrandAnn have been friends since they were kids. She lives across the street and works part-time helping GrandAnn clean the guest rooms. She is trying out for a part in an Old West–style melodrama, and she rehearses while she cleans.

She waved her dust cloth merrily.

"Going fine," she said. "I'll knock them dead."

With a second cheerful wave she disappeared

down the hall. I went back through the kitchen into Becky Thatcher and picked up my half-eaten apple. Before I could take a bite, I heard Mrs. Prescott again.

"Get away! Get away!"

The house shook with a dreadful thud.

I dropped my apple.

"Mrs. Prescott, are you all right?"

She wasn't. When I got upstairs, she was sprawled on the hallway carpet, unconscious. Beside her lay her dust rag, and scattered around her were the shards of GrandAnn's ceramic bust of Mark Twain.

As I leaned over her still body, I heard footsteps at the far end of the hall and the pounding of heavy shoes down the back stairway. The kitchen door banged.

Chapter 2

"Mrs. Prescott, can you hear me?"

She moaned and rolled her head from side to side.

"Miranda, is that you?" Her eyelids fluttered, and she struggled to sit up. "What hit me?"

"Mark Twain," I said stupidly. "I mean the statue of Mark Twain. Someone must have knocked you over the head with it."

She sat on the hallway carpet and cradled her head in her hands.

"Who on earth would do a thing like that? I can't exactly remember how it happened, Miranda, but that just doesn't seem possible. I must have hit the hall bookcase while I was practicing my part. The statue fell on me."

"You shouted for someone to get away," I said.

"Well, that proves it, then. I was rehearsing. I must have been making up lines for the melodrama."

She leaned on me heavily as I helped her to her feet. It was one of the rare times that I have been glad to be tall. I helped her along the hall to the back stairs and then down into the kitchen.

Mrs. Prescott rested by the kitchen table while I got her a glass of water and some aspirin. I wrapped ice in a dishtowel, and she held it against the swelling lump on her forehead. Orenthal, finished with his dinner, jumped into her lap, curled into a cat comma, and blessed her with a loud purr.

That's where we were when GrandAnn came in.

"Thunder, look at you!" she exclaimed. "What in the world happened?"

She bustled, brewing tea and fetching a footstool for Mrs. Prescott. The room felt warmer.

"I was rehearsing. You know how I am, Ann. I was really getting into my role, maybe a little too far into it. I knocked your bust of Mark Twain off the shelf." Her face crumpled. "I'm awfully sorry, Ann. It broke."

"That isn't important. Are you sure you don't want to go to a doctor?"

"Oh, no, Ann. Please, let's not make a fuss. I feel foolish enough already."

"I still think someone hit you."

GrandAnn stared at me. "What in thunder are you talking about?"

"Mrs. Prescott sounded like she was afraid, and then I heard someone running away, going down the back stairs."

GrandAnn looked at Mrs. Prescott. "Well?"

"No, no, no. I was alone. Probably I was just overacting." She waved her hand vaguely, as if to brush away a pesky fly. "It had to be an accident."

GrandAnn looked relieved and said, "Miranda does have a gifted imagination."

I do, but I was sure I hadn't imagined the footsteps. The main stairs from Becky Thatcher are carpeted, but the back stairs to the kitchen are bare wood. The stairwell acts like an echo chamber. I had heard someone; I was certain of it.

Besides, the bust couldn't have fallen on her head. I had dusted it last week and remembered putting it on the middle shelf. If it had fallen on her, it would have raised a knot on her toe, not on her head.

GrandAnn and Mrs. Prescott weren't taking the idea of an intruder very seriously. With an inward sigh, I decided that if anything was to be done, it would be up to me. I switched on the back porch light and looked out. There might not be anyone skulking around, but maybe there would be some clue, like footprints from those heavy shoes.

There was no sign of anything out of the ordinary. The light fell across the low shed that covers our root cellar and etched into deep shadow in the alley beyond. Just as I was going to turn the light off, out of that shadow stepped a figure.

A soft, indistinct whistle drifted across the yard, and I recognized Mr. Pitt, one of our boarders. His lips were drawn forward into a pout through which his absent-minded tune flowed. He clutched his violin case close to his chest and scowled.

Mr. Pitt played the violin at The Bard's Theater. When he was home, he was usually up in his room practicing. Actually, the two things he did most were practice his violin and scowl.

"You're just in time for dinner," I called out, as he came up the walk toward me.

He looked startled, and his scowl deepened.

"In a minute" was all he said.

He pushed past me, but stopped abruptly when he saw Mrs. Prescott. The knot on her head was swelling, and her hair hung in limp strands under the wet dishtowel. Mr. Pitt's scowl actually deepened further.

"I had a little accident, is all. I'm fine. I must have knocked something from the bookshelf onto my head."

He hadn't asked what was wrong, but he actually seemed interested in her explanation. He grunted, and trudged up the kitchen stairs toward his room, his soft whistle trailing behind him.

Mr. Pitt's room is named Pudd'nhead Wilson. He doesn't like it much. He said once that Pudd'nhead Wilson was a blasted fool, and the only worse fool he could think of was someone who thought it was cute to give a room a person's name.

Mrs. Prescott watched him start up the stairs. She looked thoughtful.

"It's the strangest thing, Ann," she said to my grandmother. "I'm just sure I know him. It's the walk, more than anything, and that strange, tuneless whistle. It can't be, though. I've never known anyone named Aloysius Pitt."

That's how I learned Mr. Pitt's first name.

Dinner was the promised quiche with apple cider and salad. GrandAnn fussed over Mrs. Prescott and chattered while she cooked. Everything seemed normal. I almost decided I really had imagined some mysterious goblin, when all along, as Dad would say, the simple explanation was the right one.

She was hit on the forehead, I thought. She would know if someone had attacked her. She would have seen the man.

Then I thought again of the pounding footsteps. They could have been made by anyone wearing boots. Or the woman, I thought, modifying my mental list of suspects.

After dinner, GrandAnn patted my shoulder briskly.

"Will you do the dishes tonight? I have to be at the city council meeting with my report, and it starts in just ten minutes."

She grabbed her jacket from the rack beside the front door, slammed a hat over her unruly hair, and blew me a kiss.

"Oh, by the way." She stopped and squinted across at the fireplace. "What goes up the chimney down but not down the chimney up?"

"An umbrella," I called out, just as the door banged and she was gone.

I put the dishes in the dishwasher under Orenthal's close supervision, then climbed the back stairs to the attic and my room.

GrandAnn's attic was originally one huge room with a high ceiling that follows the roofline of the old house. The peak is over twelve feet high, but the ceiling slants down to meet the walls just three feet from the floor.

When she found out I was coming to stay for a while, she hired carpenters to partition off a room at the end of the attic near the stairs. We call it "Miranda's Room." I insisted.

We chose white paint for the ceiling and lavender for the walls. Where the two meet, we put a border of white and purple violets. The carpet is lavender, too, and the bedspread is fake fur, as white as a snowstorm. My desk is next to a big window seat, where I can sit with the cat and read or just dream and look down on the fruit trees in the back yard and the rooftops beyond.

On my desk is a picture of my parents. Side by side, they look out at me with vast smiles. Their arms are hooked together and their heads are tipped toward each other. They are wearing fur-trimmed parkas, and behind them rises a huge white mountain.

I picked up the photograph and traced a gentle circle around my parents' faces with my finger.

No one in my family is normal, I thought. My grandmother names her rooms, and my parents skip around the world like a couple of kids.

I smiled when I thought of them, but I felt a pang, too. It was true. My parents were certainly not "normal," but I missed them more than I would ever have admitted. They always praised me for being dependable and having common sense. I could never have told them that I didn't want them to go and leave me behind.

12

Mom had written across the bottom of the picture, "Stay warm. We'll be home soon."

Mom is as tall as Dad. I couldn't see her hair in the picture, but I could imagine the long, dark brown braid hanging down her back. Dad teases her about still looking like a college student.

I have my dad's grin, but I guess I get my tallness from Mom, along with my dark brown hair. My hair is cut very short, though. I think it is a lot more practical to have short hair.

Beside the picture sits a white telephone.

"You have to go down two flights to the bathroom, but at least we can get you a telephone up here," GrandAnn had said when the phone was installed.

I hadn't wanted to mention that I didn't know anyone to call.

I could hear the soft sounds of Mr. Pitt's violin as I settled into the chair by my desk and got out my homework.

Homework! At my last school in California, we had been studying the ancient Egyptians. Here, my social studies class was learning about Oregon history. As I picked up my book, I thought that I would probably be permanently confused. By the time I was out of high school, I would think the Egyptians had dug for gold on the banks of the Rogue River and that the Forty-Niners had built pyramids on the banks of the Nile.

Mom would have described my mood as contrary. She would have been right.

I didn't really mind the homework and the confusing classes. What I did mind was that I had finally started to fit in at the school in California. Now I had a whole new set of teachers and classmates to get used to.

I also minded having my parents so very far away. They were literally at the end of the earth.

Mom and Dad are both biologists. They met each other in a college biology class. Dad likes to say that they fell in love over seaweed and pond scum.

They do a lot of field work. Their pet subject is algae, and they have to travel a lot to study it, because the most interesting kinds grow in odd places. There is even a kind that grows inside polar bear hair!

So they have to go all over the world to gather their "seaweed and pond scum" from different environments. Last year they were in Costa Rica. This year they had been sent to the South Pole, or at least close to it, to get samples of the blue-green algae of Antarctica. They wouldn't be home until May, when winter really takes hold in the Southern Hemisphere.

Mom had promised. "This is the last time."

Dad hadn't said much. He was busy with plans and packing then double-checking the plans and repacking, and then checking it all again.

"Making a list and checking it twice," he had muttered. Then he had stopped and hugged me. "One thing is certain, the time will go fast with GrandAnn. She won't bore you."

14

Dad calls her GrandAnn, too, but he got it from me. When I was little, Grandma Ann had been too hard to say, so I compressed it. Dad said it was a perfect name for her.

He always seemed to enjoy being around GrandAnn; that was for sure. They watched football games together when they could, each one trying to outdo the other in a cheering contest that usually sent Mom and me out of the room for some peace and quiet. Mom once said he only married her to have GrandAnn for a mother-in-law. Dad just grinned and winked.

My parents, like GrandAnn, can make a game out of anything. Sometimes I think I am the only responsible member of the family. It's as if I'm the grown-up, and they are all kids. As I said, it isn't normal.

Still, thinking about them almost always made me smile. I put my books aside and got out a pen and paper.

Dear Mom and Dad,

You won't believe what happened to Mrs. Prescott today . . .

Chapter 3

I must have dozed over my history book. I thought I heard my teacher from my old school in California, but her voice was coming from GrandAnn's cat. Orenthal paced in front of a world map, talking and pointing toward northern Africa with his stumpy tail.

"If the major river system in Egypt is the Nile," he said in a pompous cat-tone, "what do we call the less mature little tributaries along its length?"

I felt like a dunce. First because I didn't know the answer, and second because I was being questioned by a cat.

"I don't know," I confessed.

Orenthal wheezed a meow that could only have been cat laughter.

"Juveniles!" he shouted. "Get it, juve-*Niles!*"

He wheezed again, sounding a bit annoyed now, because I wasn't laughing at his silly joke. Then his irritated meowing shifted into a hearty yowl of protest that jerked me awake. A loud crash shook the walls.

I called out, "Who's there?"

The only answer was Orenthal's angry growl.

Cautiously I opened my bedroom door. The Jumping Frog has a stairwell between the first and second floors at both ends of the house, but there is just one flight of stairs to the third floor: the back stairs from the kitchen. The stairwells are always lighted so the guests can find their way around. That light reassured me now. No one was in sight, but Orenthal sat before my door, still growling and twitching his tail.

The rest of the attic, the part that isn't my room, is used for storage. Trunks, boxes, chairs, old bed frames, dusty rockers, and picture frames are stacked in the kind of orderly disarray that GrandAnn seems to enjoy. Windows with lace curtains contribute an odd dignity to the clutter.

It didn't take long to spot the cause of the crash. One of GrandAnn's portraits of Samuel Clemens had fallen from its hook and rested crookedly on the floor. Mr. Clemens (a.k.a. Mark Twain) wore a serious expression. The picture was tilted to the left and his face was slanted as if he had asked a question and was waiting for an answer. A diagonal crack in the glass distorted his right eye; it seemed to be winking. The whole effect was a little silly.

I felt a little silly, too. Aside from the portrait, nothing seemed to be out of place. Even Orenthal had gotten over his bad humor. He was sitting on a small braided rug and washing his tummy contentedly.

I jumped straight up when a door banged shut

downstairs, but the following silence was ruffled only by the soft, repetitive tones of Mr. Pitt's violin. I felt even sillier.

"It's just one of the guests," I muttered. "Come on, Orenthal." My voice echoed loudly. "I think it's time for a snack."

I thumped down the back stairs, pausing at the second floor to look around. The hall was empty.

"Not a guest or a gremlin, nor even a goblin in sight," I said to Orenthal, trying to sound casual and in control of the situation.

Orenthal ignored me. His green eyes glittered, and he bounded ahead, signaling me to follow with his scruffy orange tail. In the kitchen I passed over the apples and rummaged in the refrigerator until I found some fried chicken. Orenthal's tail waved his approval when I fed him a bite of skin.

I ate and thought. Obviously we didn't have gremlins or goblins, but we did have guests. Until the start of the theater season, GrandAnn had Mr. Pitt and three students from the local college boarding with her. Susan, Nick, and Julie, the students, weren't home much. They were usually away at classes, at the library, or with friends.

Mr. Pitt was there a lot, but he was usually in his room. At almost any time of the day or evening, I could hear him playing scales and practice pieces, over and over. I wasn't even aware of the sound unless I thought about it. Like now.

I tilted my head to listen. Sure enough, the faint

notes floated down the stairs. I returned to puzzling out who might have disturbed the picture.

It wasn't just a question of who. I couldn't figure out why one of the boarders might be snooping up there. It made even less sense to imagine one of them attacking poor old Mrs. Prescott.

Sometimes GrandAnn asks me a riddle that I can almost solve, but not quite. I had that same uneasy, restless feeling. My mind itched.

As I considered how a mind could itch, the phone rang.

"Miranda, this is Jessica Overstreet."

"Hi, Jessica. What's up?"

I hoped I sounded casual, but not too casual. Jessica is in my class at Branberg Middle School. The other kids look up to her, but she doesn't seem conceited. Since I had just stooped to conversing with a cat, I figured I could use a human friend.

"I wondered if you could meet Tiff and me in the library before school tomorrow. We want to interview you for the school paper."

"Sure," I said, not casually at all. "But why me?"

"Well, you're new here. It's to help people get to know you. Also, it sounds like you've been to lots of interesting places."

"Thanks. But right now this seems like a pretty interesting place to me. Do you know anything about ghosts?"

Jessica laughed. "That's a long story, but I guess the answer is no," she said. "Do you have ghost problems?"

19

"I suppose not, but things sure go bump in the night around this old house sometimes."

I told her about Mrs. Prescott and the mysterious crash upstairs. I thought she would laugh again, but she sounded serious when she answered.

"I don't know about ghosts, but if something *is* going on, be careful."

After we hung up, I wasn't sure if I felt better or not. Climbing the stairs with Orenthal close behind me, I was glad to have his company, and I was careful.

GrandAnn came up to say good night when she got home. She had a sparkle in her eye, and her hat was a bit crooked.

"It was a great meeting, Miranda. The city council wants me to start a literacy program for the itinerant workers this summer. You can help."

"What's an itinerant worker?"

I figured literacy meant reading. Since GrandAnn is a retired English teacher, that was a natural connection.

"Migrant workers. Lots of them are from Mexico. They work to harvest the crops, and they move from place to place, depending on where they are needed. It might be lettuce in California last week and strawberries in Oregon this week, and who-knows-what, who-knows-where next week. In August they will be here to harvest the pears. Lots of them don't stay in one place long enough for their children to enroll in school. I'm going to start a program to supply them with books and to make sure they all get the chance to learn to read."

GrandAnn's eyes took on a faraway gaze, as if she could see all the way to Mexico and into the minds of the children coming north to the pear orchards.

I was sympathetic. I knew how frustrating it was to move from school to school, never quite in step with the other kids. "I'll help," I offered.

She grinned. "I knew you would. You are one good kid."

She chucked me under my chin as if I were three years old. I don't mind that from her, as long as no one is looking.

"We had another mysterious occurrence," I said, trying to sound as if I was joking. "There was a crash in the attic. I think the picture of Mark Twain fell. Or else maybe it was my imaginary goblins and gremlins . . ."

A tiny frown flitted across her face as she answered, "Let's take a look."

At the stairwell, GrandAnn tugged on the string hanging from the attic ceiling bulb. Sudden brightness rushed into every corner, scattering my invisible gremlins and goblins into nothingness. I felt foolish for saying anything. Even Orenthal looked a bit sheepish.

"Thunder!" GrandAnn headed straight for the portrait of Samuel Clemens, which gazed up at us crookedly. She tilted the heavy gilt frame out from the wall and ran her hand across its back.

"Oh, no!"

A big manila envelope had been taped to the brown paper backing of the picture. GrandAnn tore it off and slipped her hand inside. It was obviously empty, but she repeated the action again and again. Finally, she ripped the brown paper backing from the frame and ran her hands across the picture itself. Then she tipped the frame back against the wall and turned to me.

Her hat was at an even crazier angle, her hair stuck out beneath it like the quills of an outraged porcupine, and the gaiety in her eyes had been replaced by something more like panic.

She focused her attention on me with a visible effort and said, through trembling lips, "It's gone!"

Chapter 4

"What? What's gone?"

"The packet of letters. The letters from Mark Twain. They're all gone."

GrandAnn sat heavily on a rocker, which responded with a puff of dust.

"It's a bit of a long story, Miranda, and I'm not even sure how much of it is true. I was waiting to tell you and your mother about it until after I had done some checking."

I must have looked *more* puzzled, not less. I certainly felt that way. She took a deep breath, settled herself in the chair, and explained.

"When I was your age, my grandmother told me about some letters. She said they were love letters to her mother, and she said they were from the great American writer, Mark Twain. She had seen them once, when she was a girl, but they had disappeared.

"I thought she was exaggerating. A wild imagination does seem to run in our family." She squeezed my hand and gave me a little smile that made me feel even closer to her.

"That's one reason I have always enjoyed Mark Twain's stories. Long before my family moved north

23

to Ashville, they ran an inn in Yreka, California. Mark Twain traveled through that area in the 1860s. My grandmother said he stayed with them, and it's certainly possible that he might have.

"My great-grandmother, Anne, would have been a young woman then. Maybe he really did take a shine to her. Maybe he really did write to her over the years. I've always enjoyed imagining that it was so."

She became silent and seemed to remember the stories told to her by her grandmother, possibly in this same room.

Attics are good places for memories, I thought.

GrandAnn stood and walked over to the old brick chimney, which was connected to the Becky Thatcher Room below.

"I'll show you a secret," she said.

She closed her eyes and lightly brushed her fingers over the rough bricks at the right edge of the chimney.

"This one," she said, opening her eyes. She grinned at me and explained. "It's smoother than the others."

She nestled her forefinger and thumb into grooves above and below the brick, then pushed it sideways. It shifted with a grating sound, then slid out of place, revealing a dark chamber within the chimney.

She had to raise herself up on tiptoe to look in, but the cavity was just below my eye level. It was about the size of six bricks, and it was lined with a shiny metal, like tin. It was empty.

"When your parents wrote to say you were coming, I could hardly wait to remodel the attic, to make a room just for you. The carpenters discovered this hiding place. It's a part of the chimney. It must have been put in when the house was built.

"The letters were here. My great-grandmother, Anne, must have hidden them to keep them safe, or maybe because they were personal."

"Were they really love letters?" I felt a little embarrassed. I wasn't sure I wanted to pry into the romantic life of one of my ancestors.

"No, not really. They were just friendly. He wrote about once a year at first, then just now and then. He explained his idea of how Yreka got its name, and he told her about his first famous story, 'The Celebrated Jumping Frog of Calaveras County.' Except it had a different title in his letter. He called it 'Jim Smiley and His Jumping Frog,' and he said he hoped it would tickle her."

"The Jumping Frog," I said. "I should have known it meant something special."

"She named the inn, you know. It's kind of nice to understand why," GrandAnn said, with a little smile. "I intended to explain it all to you and your mother as soon as I was certain the letters really were from Mark Twain.

"The first letter was dated 1865. I sent it to a woman in San Francisco who is a professional document examiner. She looks at the handwriting and the ink and paper. She can tell us if the letters are genuine."

Her smile faded as she gazed at the portrait propped against the wall.

"By the time I sent away the first letter, lots of people knew about the secret compartment, so I wanted a special hiding place. I thought it was so clever to hide the rest there, on the back of his picture."

She twisted her lips in a rueful grimace. "I can't believe I was so careless. I outsmarted myself with my silly games."

It scared me a little to see tears spill down her cheeks. Somehow it felt wrong to see an adult cry. I wished Mom and Dad were there to help, but they weren't, so I guessed it was up to me to do what I could. I wanted to fix everything for her; I wanted her to be my happy-go-lucky GrandAnn again.

"We'll get them back," I said with confidence, even though I couldn't begin to imagine how. "First, let's call the police."

The idea startled her.

"Why, yes, I suppose we must. I guess someone must have stolen them. Yes, let's call the police."

Having a plan seemed to perk her up. She wiped her eyes as she led the way down to the warm kitchen. I started water for tea while she called the city police. We waited together in Becky Thatcher, sipping herb tea sweetened with honey.

GrandAnn's thoughts seemed far away.

Finally she looked at me and asked, "What is pretty without you and pretty awful with you?"

I could hardly believe she was dreaming up

riddles at such a time. Before I could answer, the doorbell rang.

The man at the door, Officer Carlson, wore a crisp blue uniform. He had blond hair. He called GrandAnn "ma'am" in a soft, deep voice that made me believe he would have the problem solved and go on his way within an hour.

He took notes while GrandAnn described the theft. Finally, he put his pen down and asked, "Who knew about the letters?"

GrandAnn's eyebrows lifted in surprise. "Oh, dear, lots of people. When I first found them, Mrs. Prescott was here, and Julie, one of our guests, and the carpenters, and I called the head of the English department at the college, and of course I told some of my friends."

Her voice softened, and she said, with dignity, "They are all people of good character. I'm sure none of them could have stolen the letters."

"That's probably true, ma'am, but someone took them. Were any of those people especially interested in what you did with them?"

GrandAnn looked distressed. "Not that I noticed," she said.

The officer closed his notebook and sighed. "We can notify the other law enforcement agencies that the letters have been stolen. There is a chance they will turn up on the art market. I'm afraid, though, that they may be sold to a private collector. If that happens, there isn't much hope that we will recover them."

"I understand," GrandAnn said. She sat up straight, but somehow it just made her look more vulnerable. "I know you will do your best."

We stood together at the front door and watched Officer Carlson go down the walk. Then GrandAnn sighed and sank into the overstuffed chair.

"I'm truly sorry, Miranda. The letters would eventually have been yours. They were to be a surprise for you and your mother. They were like a thread between us, connecting us to each other and to our past."

I perched on the arm of her chair and rested my cheek against the top of her head. My eyes fell on the picture of Mark Twain. It was almost identical to the copy in the attic and it, too, had a gilt frame that shone softly. I smiled.

"I know. Without the *u*, gilt is pretty, but it feels awful when it's guilt."

She grinned at me. "That's it."

After a quiet moment, she shrugged as if to shake away an unhappy thought and said, "I know it isn't kind, but I confess that right now I can't help but hope that someone feels pretty awful."

Chapter 5

The hint of spring, which had beckoned GrandAnn the day before, still lingered, making the air heavy and warm as I walked to school the next morning.

I was excited about meeting with Jessica and Tiffaney, but a little nervous, too. It was true that I had lived in lots of different places, but I wasn't interested in being different. Different isn't always comfortable. I had learned that lots of times.

As I entered the school library, I vowed to be as ordinary as possible. I was relieved to see that Jessica and Tiffaney were there ahead of me. Jessica's dark curls contrasted with Tiffaney's light corn-silk hair. It was easy to see that they were friends by the way they bent toward each other as they talked. I wasn't sure I should interrupt, but just then they looked up and saw me.

"Hi!" Tiffaney waved me over.

Jessica smiled and moved over so I could sit between them. As I sat down, we were joined by another girl from our class. Georgette Jones said hi softly as she sat across from us. She twisted a lock of her brown hair around her index finger. She had a way of ducking her head when she spoke, as if she were really talking with the floor. I was glad to have her there. She made me feel less awkward.

With her pen poised above a blank sheet of notebook paper, Jessica asked her first question.

"Don't you live in that old house on Main Street, the one with the funny name?"

So much for being ordinary, I thought, but Jessica's face was so open and friendly that I tried to answer her honestly.

"Yes. It's been in our family since it was built. My grandmother runs a bed-and-breakfast there. The Jumping Frog Inn."

"An old house," Tiffaney said, sounding interested. "Is it haunted?"

"I didn't think so until yesterday," I answered. Then, seeing the looks on their faces, I explained.

"I don't get it," Jessica said. "Why would anyone steal a bunch of letters?"

"Partly because they're worth money. People like to collect things written by anyone famous. GrandAnn says their greatest value is to people who study history and writing. The letters show what Mark Twain was thinking about and might tell something about how he wrote his stories."

"If anyone can help you, Jess can," Georgette said, with a smile that danced across her face and made her suddenly seem very pretty. She's the sleuth of the group!"

"I'll try," Jessica said, smiling back. "Do you have any suspects?"

"I figure it must be one of the guests. It couldn't

be Mrs. Prescott because I don't see how she could have hit herself on the head. Besides, I heard her shouting 'Get away!' at someone, and I'm sure someone ran down the stairs after she was attacked."

"Tell us about the guests." Tiffaney tipped her head to the left as she spoke, and I had a sudden image of the crooked picture.

I shuddered. Someone really had been in the attic. The thief must have been just a few feet away while I was dreaming that crazy dream about Orenthal. Probably that same person had hurt Orenthal. Probably he, or she, would have been willing to hurt me as well, if I had been in the way.

Jessica took notes while I counted off the guests.

"During the season when the theater is closed, GrandAnn takes in boarders. Right now we have Mr. Pitt and three college students: Susan, Nick, and Julie."

I borrowed Jessica's pen and drew a map of the second floor of GrandAnn's house. "The two rooms at the back are Huckleberry Finn and Pudd'nhead Wilson."

I stopped when I caught their puzzled expressions. They probably thought I had lost my grip on reality. Quickly I explained about the custom of naming rooms in a bed-and-breakfast and how GrandAnn had chosen Mark Twain characters. Jessica and Georgette seemed to understand, but Tiffaney still looked uncertain. I decided not to mention that the living room was named Becky.

31

"Anyway, a college student named Julie lives in Huck Finn. Mr. Pitt, a musician for The Bard's Theater, lives in Pudd'nhead Wilson."

They accepted that, so I went on.

"At the front we have Tom Sawyer and The Connecticut Yankee. Tom is opposite Huck Finn, and Susan lives there."

I closed my eyes to concentrate better.

"Across from Pudd'nhead Wilson is The Connecticut Yankee. That's from *The Connecticut Yankee in King Arthur's Court*," I explained hastily. "Nick lives there —"

"Planning a party?"

"What? Oh, no. I was just . . ."

I looked up and blushed at the sight of Tim and Josh, two of the cutest boys in the whole school.

Why did I get such fair skin? Blushes make me look like a summer sunset. I studied the table so my face wouldn't light up the room, and I heard Jessica come to my rescue.

"Hi, Tim. Hi, Josh. Miranda was just explaining who lives where in her grandmother's inn."

I looked up to find her grinning at me. I guess it *had* sounded a little like the guest list at a costume party.

The boys sat on either side of Georgette. Either they hadn't noticed my red face, or they pretended not to. They actually looked interested when Jessica explained about the letters.

"Were you scared?" Tim asked me seriously.

Suddenly I realized that I had been scared. Part

of me still was, scared for me and, even more, scared for GrandAnn.

"Yes," I admitted. "I think I still am."

Jessica made more notes while I told them what I knew about our boarders.

"Julie is nice but she's pretty serious. She studies a lot because she wants to get into medical school. She eats most of her meals away and spends almost every evening in the lab at the biology building. She's friendly enough, but she almost never talks about herself."

I pictured Julie, blond and slender, tossing her hair back as she ran up the stairs. "She's pretty," I added.

"Who else?" Josh was leaning forward on his elbows as if I were his favorite television show. I rushed ahead to keep from blushing again.

"Well, there's Mr. Pitt in Pudd'nhead Wilson."

I avoided Tim's puzzled gaze.

"He hates it. He says Pudd'nhead is a foolish name for a grown man."

A sudden memory made me smile. "Mr. Pitt's first name is Aloysius."

"I suppose they call him Al," Tiffaney said.

I tried to imagine that, but couldn't, so I went on.

"Nick is really friendly. He's always hanging around the kitchen when he's home. He likes GrandAnn's cat, and sometimes he even lets Orenthal sleep in his room."

"Orenthal?"

Josh couldn't help asking, I guess.

33

"The cat. It's some kind of a riddle. GrandAnn loves riddles. I haven't figured that one out yet.

"Anyway, I think Nick is really nice. I don't see how he could be the thief."

"Is he cute?" Tiffaney wanted to know.

"I guess so. He's kind of old."

"Honestly!" Jessica said, and rolled her eyes at Tiffaney in an exaggerated gesture. "Let me finish my list, Tiff."

Georgette giggled.

"Susan is in Tom Sawyer. I don't really trust her. She's standoffish. Mostly I see her carrying huge stacks of books up to her room, and she is always slamming doors.

"She seems to be a Mark Twain fan, too. She said she was glad to be in the Tom Sawyer Room, and she asked to have the attic picture of Mark Twain moved into her room even though the glass was cracked. I think she was miffed when GrandAnn said no."

"That could be it! She was after the letters. I'll bet if we searched her room we would find them." Jessica was so excited she almost squealed. She scribbled stars by Susan's name on her list.

It was Tiffaney's turn to roll her eyes, but she was smiling.

Georgette didn't smile, though. She pushed her glasses up on her nose with her thumb, twisted her lips crookedly, and blinked. She looked uncomfortable. "Maybe she's just shy," she said.

I tried to imagine Susan as shy, but failed. She was far too abrupt and superior acting for that. Then I remembered something else.

"She hates Orenthal. One day she found him in her room, and she screamed until I rescued him."

"Would she know about the letters?" Josh wondered.

"I think everyone knew but me. GrandAnn announced it to the world when she found them."

Jessica had four names on her list. She hesitated, then added Mrs. Prescott. She laid her pencil diagonally across the notebook paper and sat back in her chair.

"It adds up to zero," she said. "We need to know more."

"Meanwhile," Tiffaney added, "we were going to interview Miranda for the paper, and —"

The bell interrupted her. While we scrambled for our books, Jessica bent to peer closely at one of the library shelves.

"Speaking of *The Tragedy of Pudd'nhead Wilson*," she said, "here it is. I think I'll read it for my English project."

She grabbed the book and stopped to check it out, calling over her shoulder, "Let's finish the interview tomorrow."

I was at my seat in science class before I realized how good I felt. They had actually accepted me and been interested in my mystery. Maybe this year wasn't going to be a total disaster after all.

I could hardly believe it when the teacher, Mr. Stallworth, started the day by asking us a riddle.

"What's the oldest thing at the bottom of the ocean?"

It was Georgette who had the answer.

"Tyrannosaurus wrecks."

Chapter 6

"I heard it from my little brothers," Georgette explained. "They like corny jokes, and they like dinosaurs." When she found out that the inn was just three blocks from her house, she had suggested we walk to school and back together.

Our shoes hit the pavement in unison, tapping out a paired rhythm. I realized how much I had missed having a friend.

Georgette's hair had appeared just-plain-brown in the school library, but outdoors it picked up sunbeams and played with them. When I looked closely, her smile hinted of mischief, and her giggle was contagious. Her voice was quiet, and when she giggled, she swallowed a lot of the sound so it came out like the echo of a hiccup. That made me laugh even harder.

She was very quiet when I talked about my parents' job and how it took them away. She told me that her dad was getting her contact lenses for her birthday in two months. She didn't say much else about her family, just that she couldn't stay long because she had to take care of her two brothers, who were twins, and a little sister.

"I know how it feels," I told her. "GrandAnn needs

me to help out, and when my parents are home, they're always busy, and I have to do a lot of the chores and cooking."

The distance to GrandAnn's house seemed too short. I was sorry when we turned the corner onto Main Street. The inn dominated the neighborhood. Crisp white paint, accented with what GrandAnn called "dignified green," made the house seem self-confident. The ornate sign on the front lawn announced:

JUMPING FROG INN
Bed-and-Breakfast
Conversation Optional

We went through the front door into the Becky Thatcher Room. GrandAnn and Mrs. Prescott were there, drinking tea out of delicate china cups. The cups were white with pale pink roses, and I thought they perfectly suited GrandAnn's delicate features. Mrs. Prescott would have looked more at home with a sturdy mug. Her lively manner and hearty laugh reassured me that she had recovered from her adventure with Mark Twain.

"GrandAnn, this is Georgette," I said.

"I'm very happy to meet you," GrandAnn said with just the right amount of enthusiasm. I had been a little afraid she would sound too relieved that I had finally found a friend.

Mrs. Prescott held out a plate of cookies and said,

"Hi, Georgette. Have an apple spice cookie, freshly baked."

"Hello, Mrs. Prescott," Georgette answered. She smiled as she reached for a cookie and said, "Thank you."

"Do you already know each other?" I asked.

"Oh, mercy me, yes!" Mrs. Prescott exclaimed. "In a small town, you get so you know everyone after a while, and I've lived in Ashville forever. Even before she started school, your grandmother and I built forts in the heaps of dirt left over by the gold miners. I've known most of the folks around here since they were born, including this one."

She blessed Georgette with a warm smile and urged her to take a second cookie.

Georgette and I left the women to their tea and took our cookies up to the attic. I showed her the picture of Mark Twain. Then I had her close her eyes and stroke the chimney bricks until she located the smooth one. Her eyes reflected a glint of delight when she slid the brick aside, revealing the secret niche.

"That's a perfect hiding place," she said. "Are there any other hidden chambers or passages in this house?"

"Not that I know of . . ." I started to answer.

The idea made me feel kind of creepy. I decided to ask GrandAnn about it.

Georgette suddenly leaned toward the window and pulled the lace curtain aside. I followed her gaze out across the back yard toward the alley.

"Who is that?"

"Mr. Pitt. What in the world is he doing in the shed?"

The answer was obvious. He held a paper bag against his chest. Apples overflowed from the bag, and from the way he clutched its lumpy bottom, it looked very heavy. He peered up and down the alley, then dashed out to his car, opened the door, and dumped the bag on the front seat. He ducked in and drove off.

I was a little embarrassed. I was sure no one minded his having the apples, but he looked so shifty. I was grateful when Georgette changed the subject.

"I'll come by tomorrow morning, and we can walk to school together," she said. "Let's leave a few minutes early so we can meet Tiff and Jess before the bell."

We clattered down the back stairs. GrandAnn and Mrs. Prescott had finished their tea and were playing checkers at the kitchen table.

"Come again," GrandAnn said to Georgette as we passed through the kitchen.

It felt good to hear Georgette reply, "Thanks, I will."

We stopped by the shed to say goodbye. Georgette was the first to notice the door.

"He left it open," she said.

Sure enough, the shed door stood ajar, revealing the dark interior. GrandAnn might think I had left it open, and that irritated me.

40

Some adults are as careless as kids, I thought, as I grabbed the edge of the door and shoved.

"What's in there?"

"It's just a root cellar." I reversed the direction of the door and opened it wider. We peered in.

"GrandAnn uses it mostly to store fruit from her trees. It's dug down into the earth and that keeps it from getting too hot or too cold."

I bent my head to get through the low door, then stepped inside with Georgette close behind.

The shed's roof is low, but just inside the door, a set of open wooden steps leads down. Even Georgette had to duck to get through the doorway, but once down on the second step she could easily straighten up.

"Gosh," she said. "It's dark."

"And deep," I added, then looked up at the ceiling. "And cobwebby."

There were no windows. The only light came through the open door behind us. Shelves on each side of the cramped walkway held baskets and jars of food, mostly apples, pears, and root crops like potatoes and carrots. I could dimly see the back wall about fifteen feet in front of me as I stood on the bottom step. Darkness swallowed all the detail. The light from the open door shifted as Georgette moved from side to side in back of me. Shadows jumped up, then shrank back.

Gremlins and goblins, I couldn't help thinking, and once they were in my mind it was hard to

41

banish them. Or at least spiders . . . big spiders . . . spiders the size of basketballs.

Light would have helped, but there was no light. I wanted to get out of there. I wanted to get out of there right away!

Thank goodness, Georgette had the same idea. She was already ducking out into the afternoon sunshine. I followed and pushed the door shut, hard. The February sun was still bright, but some of its warmth had faded while we were in the shed.

I looked at Georgette and shook my shoulders, as if to shake off cobwebs. She did the same. That brought us both back into the everyday world, and we laughed, but the laughter sounded a little shaky.

I slipped the metal hasp into place and hooked the padlock through it. I didn't snap the lock shut. I didn't even know if we had a key for it. GrandAnn says that if anyone needs to steal food, they are welcome to it. We just close the door to keep out animals and weather.

I felt a prickle of relief with the door firmly shut. Georgette sighed as if she felt it, too.

"That would be a perfect home for goblins and gremlins," I said, giving voice to my silly imaginings.

"At least they wouldn't be hungry," Georgette offered.

A disgusting thought wormed its way into my mind. I just couldn't keep from saying it aloud. "Especially if they like to eat spiders."

Georgette's nose wrinkled and her eyes widened

in mock horror. Then she grinned. "That reminds me. I have to get home. It's late and I have to get dinner started."

She called back over her shoulder as she hurried down the alley. "I'll be by at seven-thirty."

GrandAnn and Mrs. Prescott were still bent over the checkerboard when I returned to the kitchen. Cozy, I thought, and I was thankful for it.

I refused GrandAnn's offer of another cookie, but I couldn't resist asking her a riddle. "What did the mother gremlin say to her baby at the dinner table?"

GrandAnn looked blank, then she wrinkled her nose in an unconscious imitation of Georgette. "Quit goblin your food."

Before she had a chance to counter with a riddle of her own, the kitchen door banged open and Susan hurried in.

Chapter 7

"Oh, hi," she said. Her dark eyebrows lifted, and she drew away from me slightly, as if I were covered with thorns and she feared getting too close. She seemed surprised to see us, but Susan usually seemed surprised when her concentration was interrupted by people. "I just wondered whether it's all right if I make a sandwich."

I watched Susan slam peanut butter on bread and tried not to notice when she opened a can of sardines and placed the little creatures tenderly across the top. It almost seemed tastier to imagine a party of goblins in the shed, celebrating the darkness with a feast of spiders and apples.

Susan didn't say more. Her eyebrows were back in their normal position, forming a low black line above her eyes as she grabbed the sandwich and a stack of books and headed up the back stairs to the Tom Sawyer Room.

I tried on the idea that she had been rude because she felt guilty, but I had to admit that she had mostly just acted like Susan. When she left, Orenthal rubbed against my legs, fussing. I assumed he was discussing the sardines, and I poured the leftover juice into his dish.

"It's an awful shame about your grandmother's letters."

I wasn't sure if Mrs. Prescott was talking to me or to GrandAnn, but I was glad she had brought up the subject.

"It's just hard for me to imagine that someone actually took them," GrandAnn said, sounding as if her last friend had left her.

I couldn't help contributing. "I think it must be Mr. Pitt." I met their serious faces bravely. "I see him sneaking around," I said, thinking of the way he had looked with his bag of apples.

They didn't respond, so I went on. "He isn't very friendly."

Still no response.

"It has to be someone who lives here."

"Officer Carlson said he would talk to all the guests today," GrandAnn said. "Maybe he can learn something constructive."

I got the message. My ideas were less than constructive. Still, I couldn't shake the feeling that Mr. Pitt was up to something.

I was searching for a way to explain my feelings when Mrs. Prescott leaned forward and said, in a stage whisper, "Maybe it was Susan. It's kind of hard to trust someone who hates cats and eats peanut butter with" — she paused dramatically — "sardines!"

It was so close to what I had been thinking that I had to laugh. Even GrandAnn smiled, so I decided to try again.

"Maybe she's right. We know that Susan is crazy about Mark Twain. I think you should have her room searched."

"I'm afraid we need more to go on than an aversion to cats and a fondness for literature," GrandAnn said. "The police need hard evidence. We don't have any."

GrandAnn's usual sparkle had faded, but her mood lightened when we started to fix dinner. Mrs. Prescott distracted us both by describing, with dramatic emphasis, her part in the melodrama.

"It's set in the gold rush days," she said. "There is an evil landlord who wants to evict the heroine, even though there is a storm blowing outside and she has no coat or shoes. My role is the mother of the heroine. I wear a huge floppy hat and wring my hands and cry a lot."

"What's this about the police?"

We were so intent on Mrs. Prescott's story that we all jumped. Nick stood at the swinging door between the kitchen and the Becky Thatcher Room. His hair is just a little curly. Usually it falls back in deep waves from his forehead, and his eyes normally twinkle. But now he strode into the room with a hard glint in his eyes and his hair straight up, as if he had combed it with a rake.

He practically shouted at GrandAnn, "I hear the police were here last night! Why?"

Before she could answer, he flopped into a chair and pushed his fingers through his hair, stirring it

46

into an unruly tangle. He took a deep breath, then another.

"I'm sorry. I didn't mean to shout. Did they ask about me?"

"No, Nick. It's not about you."

Evidently GrandAnn wasn't as surprised as I was.

"Some of my personal property was taken," she said. "I had to report it."

She went on to explain about the letters and told him that Officer Carlson would contact him, but only about whether he had seen anyone or anything suspicious.

I stayed very quiet. I certainly did not want to be sent out of the room until I discovered what was bothering Nick.

He started to relax a little. "I guess I overreacted, Ann. It just seems that every time something happens, people point at me."

He reached down and scratched Orenthal under the chin briefly. Orenthal yawned widely and waited for a moment. Then, when the supply of attention dwindled, he strolled out beneath the swinging door.

"I had enough trouble with that deal back in high school. I don't need any more, especially now. I'm sorry about your letters, Ann. Is there anything I can do to help?"

GrandAnn asked him a lot of questions, but his answers boiled down to the general conclusion that Nick was out of the house a lot more than he was in

47

it. When he was home, he was usually in his room and hadn't observed anything unusual.

"I feel like I ought to be of some use, though," he said, with a smile that made him seem more like the Nick I thought I knew. "After all, I do live in Connecticut Yankee. I should protect you fair damsels like the knights of yore."

"The knights of our what?" GrandAnn said teasingly.

And then we heard the scream.

It echoed through the upstairs hall and down the stairwell. GrandAnn led the way. She was the first one up the stairs, closely followed by Nick, then me, then Mrs. Prescott. We scrambled down the hallway in a blizzard of pounding hearts and pounding feet.

GrandAnn arrived at Susan's door and stopped so abruptly that Nick, then I, then Mrs. Prescott skidded into her.

"Oh, dear. Let me take him."

GrandAnn reached out, then turned to us with Orenthal clutched securely in her arms. Her lips were firmly pressed together, and she was frowning so deeply that I was sure she was trying to stifle a guffaw.

She thrust Orenthal into Nick's arms and said, "Evidently Orenthal doesn't object to peanut butter with his sardines."

Her speech was punctuated by the bang of Susan's door slamming shut.

We paraded down the hall in reverse order and

returned to the kitchen, where Nick banished Orenthal into temporary exile in the back yard.

His step was light as he came back into the kitchen and, with a silly smirk, he said, "Hey, Ann, Orenthal wants to know. If the emperor of Russia was called a tsar, and the empress was called a tsarina, what did they call their children?"

"That's an old one, Nick," GrandAnn said, as she set spoons and forks beside the plates on the table. Her eyes gleamed with merriment as she answered, "A tsardine."

After dinner GrandAnn and I sat together in Becky Thatcher. The episode with Orenthal had restored the usual sunshine to her mood. I decided to try one more time.

"GrandAnn, I think we should search all the rooms."

She actually laughed. "We can't do that, Miranda. Even the police would need a search warrant. Besides, I trust our guests. They wouldn't hurt me."

"How about Nick?" I couldn't help asking. "It sounds like he isn't so trustworthy."

"Nick was in trouble three years ago, but it's behind him now. He was with some other boys and they took a car. I guess they call it 'joy riding.' An older boy was driving, which doesn't make Nick any less at fault, but the judge gave him probation. I've been working with his probation officer. Nick is

49

doing well at the college and soon he will earn his degree."

The big chair made her look especially fragile and doll-like. When she settled back in it, her feet dangled above the floor. "Actually, he is planning to work with kids in trouble. I don't think he has any real harm in him, and he has a whole lot of real good."

"Sometimes I think you are too trusting, GrandAnn."

She blew me a kiss and answered. "That is a flaw that I would be proud to have."

Chapter 8

The next morning, Orenthal wasn't in the kitchen demanding breakfast. I searched all of his usual cat hideaways.

He wasn't in a closet, inspecting the dark corners. He wasn't in a hallway, playing tag with phantom friends. He wasn't hiding under a bed, as Tom Sawyer's cat had done, nor on the stairs, nor in the attic, nor outside in the yard.

"I think Susan did something to Orenthal," I announced when I returned to the kitchen. "She hates him."

"Some people are truly terrified of cats," GrandAnn said. "If she feels that way, she would be the last person to hurt him. She wouldn't go near him."

GrandAnn can stick up for anyone.

Orenthal still hadn't appeared when Georgette arrived at the kitchen door. I picked up my books, blew GrandAnn a kiss, and Georgette and I started out for the alley. When we passed the root cellar, a strange sound stopped us.

Thump. Thump.

We both looked around. A hollow, rhythmic sound was coming from the shed.

Thump.

I pulled the padlock out of the hasp and tugged the door aside.

Orenthal stalked out. He glared straight ahead. His tail vibrated as if with fury at the entire flea-bitten, mouse-famished, bath-taking world.

He marched haughtily to the back door with us close behind. I opened the kitchen door for him, and he stepped through, dripping dignity. Georgette and I could hear GrandAnn fussing over him all the way back down the walk.

Georgette had laughed at Orenthal's ultradignified return to the house, but when we passed the shed again she looked puzzled and said, "The door was fastened. How did he get in there?"

I wondered, too.

I was still a little worried about the interview for the school paper, but walking with Georgette I felt less like an outsider. I heard Tiffaney giggling before we even got through the library door.

They were sitting at the same table in the library, with Josh and Tim and a newcomer, a boy named Steve. Jessica waved us over. As we settled into chairs and spread out our gear, the librarian looked up and smiled at us, then went back to shelving books.

I tried saying hello, but it came out in a whisper. I cleared my throat and finally managed to say hi loudly enough to be heard.

"You know Steve, don't you?" Tim asked. "He begged us to let him come along."

Tim looked startled when Steve's elbow landed in his ribs. I felt myself blush.

"Honestly!" Jessica said, and rummaged through her notebook for her list of questions.

Tiffaney was putting film into a camera. "So we can put your picture with the interview," she explained.

Jessica started the questioning.

"Why did your family move to Ashville?" she asked, then she faltered. "I mean, why did you move to Ashville by yourself? Or rather, what made you come to stay with your grandmother . . ."

She looked more uncomfortable each time she rephrased the question. Tiffaney chimed in.

"Jess wants to ask you to tell us something about yourself and how you came to be with us," she said.

Jessica shot her a grateful look.

"Well, my parents are in Antarctica right now," I said. "They're on a government expedition."

Jessica scribbled notes busily, looking a bit relieved that I hadn't been offended by her awkward questions. Georgette listened with a serious expression, and I didn't dare look at the boys. Tiffaney's reaction was the one I enjoyed.

"You mean they're actually at the South Pole?" she said, with amazement all over her face. "How incredibly romantic!"

"Not right at the pole, but close," I answered. "They study algae — seaweed and stuff. They're phycologists.

53

"Maybe it is romantic. They seem to have a lot of fun together. Anyway, they are collecting samples of blue-green algae for some environmental study the government is doing."

"How long will they be gone?" Jessica asked.

"Until May. But they say we won't be moving again. They're going to find a house in Ashville. That's why they sent me here, to get started in school. Usually they take me with them. I went to Africa with them when I was little."

"What kind of schools did they have there?" Josh asked.

"Well, I didn't actually go to school. My parents taught me at home."

I looked at the three girls. Here it was. I was taller than Jessica and Georgette, and at least as tall as Tiffaney, but now came the part that might keep them from truly being my friends. I took a breath and continued.

"That's why I'm young for my grade. My folks sort of overdid it, and by the time we got back to the States, I was put ahead a grade."

Six pairs of eyes watched me. I wanted to disappear. It was bad enough to have been all over the world by the age of ten, and to be living in a place called The Jumping Frog, for heaven's sake. Even my height and my acting as old as I could wasn't going to change my actual age.

I was temporarily rescued by the basketball coach, who picked the perfect moment to stick his head in the door, and say, "Boys, I need to see you about a change in the practice schedule."

Josh and Tim jumped up, and Steve followed more slowly. As they left I realized he hadn't said a word.

As I sorted through ways to change the subject, Tiffaney cocked her head in her almost comic way and asked me a direct question.

"Well, how old are you?"

There was no way to avoid it.

"Eleven." It sounded so babyish. "I won't be twelve until next June."

"Wow!" she said. "You're the most interesting thing that has happened around here since Jess's hill was haunted. This is going to be a great story for the paper."

"Jessica, you don't have to tell them I'm so young, do you?" I asked, trying to sound as though it didn't really matter.

"Not if you don't want me to," Jessica said, then added, "I'll make a deal with you. I won't tell, if you'll call me Jess."

Before I could react, Tiffaney pointed her camera across the table at me, and there was an instant of dazzling light. I was still blinking when the bell rang.

"Me, too. I'm Tiff to my friends," Tiffaney — no — Tiff said.

Later, while Mr. Stallworth took roll, Georgette leaned over and whispered, "I definitely don't go by George."

I didn't think about the letters or Orenthal all
morning. I thought about Tiff and Jess and Georgette. I thought about Tim and Josh and Steve. Most
of all, I thought about how I was beginning to really
enjoy Ashville.

I especially enjoyed the note GrandAnn had left
on the table for me when I got home.

> Dear Grandchild,
>
> Don't worry about me or the mystery of
> the missing mail. Don't search anything but
> Miranda's Room.
>
> You are looking for a cross between a
> dog and a vegetable. Happy hunting!

She didn't sign it. She didn't need to.

Chapter 9

I skipped up the stairs to my room with a new feeling of lightness. Even Orenthal seemed to be in an improved mood after his escape that morning. He didn't skip, but he did leap from step to step with unusual cheerfulness.

I swung open the door to my room and laughed out loud. I should have known. There was a cauliflower on my desk. Under it was a second note. I picked it up and read it, still smiling.

> You know that you will always be
> The apple of my eye.
> If you will fetch the apples home,
> I'll make the apple pie.

I changed into my old jeans and my most beat-up shoes, and put on a sweatshirt that read Property of the University of Oregon. The slurred sounds of Mr. Pitt's violin contrasted with the staccato of raindrops striking the roof and windows.

I missed the sunshine, but after all it was still February, still winter here. And still summer at the South Pole, I thought, missing my folks even more than the sunshine.

I sat in the window seat and watched the sheets of rain pour down the glass. Peace washed over me, like the rain over the window. I felt safe, as if the attic was my private sanctuary.

The daffodils that lined the back walk nodded their heads, pushed down by the heavy drops. They reminded me a little of GrandAnn, bowing her head to the loss of her precious letters.

Remembering GrandAnn's loss cut into my still mood. We weren't safe, really. Someone had hurt GrandAnn, and that same person had invaded this attic sanctuary while I slept. The peace drifted away and left me feeling angry and vulnerable.

I carried the cauliflower down to the kitchen. This time Orenthal led the way. He knows where we keep the kitty snacks.

I shrugged a rain jacket over my sweatshirt and grabbed a canvas tote bag for the apples. The rain had intensified and the gray of the sky had shifted to a darker shade. When I opened the back door, it seemed that the rain was actually trying to get into the house. Tugging the door firmly shut, I scurried across to the shed.

Automatically, I reached for the hanging padlock, but my fingers touched only the rusty hasp.

The padlock wasn't there. The moment of surprise I felt quickly gave way to irritation. Probably Mr. Pitt had been after more apples. I swung the door open, peered into the gloom, then stepped in and down the narrow stairs.

Shelves of worn wooden slats loomed up on either side of me, rising up all the way to the ceiling. The top two shelves held only dust and litter. At eye level, baskets full of apples stood in orderly rows, like cancan dancers. Red, green, yellow, and speckled apples filled the air with a scent that reminded me of autumn. The lower shelves held jars of home-preserved fruits and vegetables from GrandAnn's back-yard garden. Peaches, tomatoes, pickles, relish, apricots, pears, and GrandAnn's own special recipe, Piccalilli Piquant, filled dusty jars.

I wished for a flashlight. The dark corners shimmered faintly with spider webs and heaven-knows-what. A thin shaft of light crept in between two boards on my left, but it only made the rest of the shed seem darker. The floor sloped gradually down into a deeper gloom until, at the very back, darkness hid everything. The rain made a hollow sound, splattering against the roof like marbles dropped on a library floor.

I grabbed a handful of green Newtown apples and dropped them, not too gently, into the canvas bag. My second handful was too ambitious and one apple escaped. It rolled when it hit the floor and landed in a dark corner under the bottom shelf.

"Oh no, you don't," I said aloud, wishing GrandAnn were there to hear my joke. "You aren't going to desert my dessert."

The silly pun made me feel braver as I squatted to peer under the shelf. A metallic glint caught my eye. The apple had come to rest against something shiny. Curiosity made me braver still, and I stretched my hand out to pick up the apple.

A key glistened against the dusty floor. I grabbed it and slipped it into my jeans pocket with the vague idea that it might be for the missing padlock.

The wind, gaining strength, pushed at the door. The light dimmed, then brightened, then dimmed again. Shadows writhed. I suddenly wanted very badly to be out of there.

I grabbed a dozen more apples and turned to dash out into the rain. As I clattered up the steps I heard a sound behind me, coming from the farthest recesses of the cellar.

Tap, tap, tap. In quick succession, again, tap, tap, tap. The sound, like metal striking stone, seemed to come out of the earth behind the back wall.

In an instant, my imagination created graves in the back yard, with long-dead pioneers struggling to escape through our root cellar. I saw the wall tremble, then shift slightly, as if someone, or something, were trying to come through.

I'm afraid I screamed.

Chapter 10

"Could it be the famous imagination of Miranda B. Caldwell?" GrandAnn asked.

I think she was trying to take me seriously. But even I had to admit that creeping shadows and mysterious underground tapping lost their effect in the warm kitchen. I held out the key.

"What about this?"

She turned it over slowly, squinting at the numbers.

"It's a palindrome," she said.

"What does a palindrome unlock?" I asked.

"Actually, it's an odd key, like one to an old-fashioned lock," she said, "but the palindrome part isn't the key itself. The palindrome is the number on the top. It's 2112. That reads the same backward and forward. Like *wow,* or *aha,* or —"

"Or like 'Madam, I'm Adam,' " I said, remembering the idea but not the word.

"That's it," GrandAnn said brightly, changing the subject even further away from ghastly noises and ghostly shadows. "Did you find the book?"

My blank look made her smile.

"You were too distracted by goblins. I put a new

copy of *A Connecticut Yankee in King Arthur's Court* out there for you. Let's go get it."

I was reaching for the doorknob when the kitchen door burst open. Susan stood there, drenched.

"I hate this rain," she said angrily.

Her black hair was plastered to her head. Her cheeks were mottled with red splotches. She pushed into the room and glared at me and GrandAnn. "I hate this rain," she repeated, then she stomped up the back stairway.

GrandAnn gave me a look that said, "Watch out, she's mad and wet."

She handed me a flashlight. I muttered, "Thanks," and glanced at it, then looked closer. A cartoon-type figure of a grinning lightning bug was embossed on the handle. It was just the kind of thing I would expect to find in GrandAnn's house.

The rain didn't feel so cold and wet with the light in my hand and, more importantly, with GrandAnn beside me. The shed looked ordinary, even a little shabby. It certainly wasn't threatening, at least until I tried to open the door. The padlock was back!

"Honest, GrandAnn, it really wasn't here," I said, but I wouldn't have blamed her if she thought I was making up the whole thing. "Maybe it was Susan. She just came from out here."

"Or maybe," she said, "Susan noticed the lock was missing and put it back. She might have done us a favor, Miranda. Don't be too ready to blame her just because you don't like her."

I shined the light around the shelves and quickly

located the book in a basket of yellow apples. We stopped to listen for the tapping sound, but we only heard the rain tapping on the roof.

Back in the kitchen, GrandAnn started her pie crust, and I sat at the table, losing myself in the adventures of Hank Morgan, the Connecticut Yankee who was carried back through time to the Middle Ages.

Mrs. Prescott knocked at the kitchen door, then bustled in, full of stories about her rehearsal. She and GrandAnn settled into gentle chatter as they peeled and sliced apples. Mr. Pitt's violin sweetened the air, and the kitchen radio provided another layer of background noise.

All the guests were there for dinner that night, and GrandAnn asked Mrs. Prescott to stay, too. Mr. Pitt was the first one at the table.

"What's all this fuss with the police?" he asked. "I must warn you, Ann, that I expect to be allowed my privacy. If this keeps up I will have to move, and I will complain to the chamber of commerce that your inn is an unsavory place, a place where criminals are sheltered."

He picked up his napkin, shook it out with a loud snap, and placed it on his lap. Nick and Julie arrived in the middle of his speech, and he glared at them as if they were examples of what he had been talking about.

Before GrandAnn could answer him, Julie spoke up. "It isn't Ann's fault, you know. I think we should help her get her letters back instead of making things harder for her. The police are only here to help."

Nick sat silently, studying his fork as if he was trying to memorize the pattern. He looked up as Susan came in and dropped into the chair beside him, then he went back to concentrating on the fork.

I helped GrandAnn serve beef stew and salad, then she asked who wanted apple pie. Nick and Mrs. Prescott had ice cream with theirs. Julie had a slice of cheddar cheese. Susan, GrandAnn, and I had ours plain. Mr. Pitt refused, making a bad joke about Adam and Eve and saying he preferred to avoid apples.

"I suppose the police have talked to all of you by now," GrandAnn said as she sat down again.

Silence seeped into the room and filled it.

"I know I was foolish to keep the letters here, but they had been hidden in this house for so many years. I just assumed they would be safe." She paused, folding and refolding her napkin. Finally she looked up with shining eyes. "I just wanted to be able to look at them and touch them. They meant a lot to me."

"Foolishness is right," Mr. Pitt said gruffly. "Plain foolishness not to put them in a secure place, like a safe deposit box. Believe me, living here, I keep all my valuables in a safe deposit box at the bank. It's foolishness to take chances with the crime rate up every year."

He glared at Nick again.

"I know that, now," GrandAnn said, looking even

more stricken. "I'm sorry if it has caused you any trouble. I hope none of you think you're being accused of taking the letters."

She looked at Nick, too, but her look was full of gentleness and encouragement. Nick just hung his head miserably.

"I suppose they're worth a lot of money," Julie said thoughtfully. "Maybe someone wants a reward for their return. Or maybe someone just wants to keep them, like a collector, or a Mark Twain fan."

I watched Susan. She shifted in her chair uncomfortably and avoided looking at GrandAnn.

GrandAnn studied her napkin again. "That's what concerns me. If someone wants them, as I did, just to keep as a way of being close to a great figure in literature, then we will probably never see them again."

"How can we help you?" Nick asked, breaking his silence.

She smiled up at him. "It would mean a lot to me and Miranda if you could just tell us if you notice anything or think of anything that might help. Oh, that reminds me. We found this key in the root cellar. Does it belong to any of you?"

She held up the brass key. Mrs. Prescott gasped. We all turned to stare at her, which flustered her even more.

"Oh, dear," she said. "It just reminded me, for a second, of my father. He had a key like that for the old metal box where he kept what he called his 'vallables,' things like birth certificates and a bit of

65

gold dust, and the like." She dabbed at her eyes with her napkin and added, "His will was in that strongbox. That's where we found it when he passed on, bless his old bones."

GrandAnn rose and put the key on the counter, then bent over Mrs. Prescott and put a gentle arm around her shoulder.

"Who wants another piece of pie?" GrandAnn asked, in a cheerful attempt to change our mood. "Thunder! The trees produced enough apples this year to make a hundred pies. We don't want them to go to waste."

No one responded. GrandAnn's sunny smile stiffened a little, and she started to clear plates from the table. Julie rose to help her. The rest of us sat quietly, each of us lost in private thoughts.

"We interrupt our normal programming to bring you this special announcement." The radio played softly, but in the silence the announcer caught our attention. Mr. Pitt reached over the counter and turned up the volume. I think we were all glad for the distraction.

"The intersection of Main and Agate streets has been made impassable by a cave-in. Motorists are advised to find alternate routes. The cave-in, which started at four o'clock this afternoon, has been steadily growing larger. As of six-thirty this evening, it measures ten feet across, and the edges are still crumbling. Chief of police Norman Wells says the recent rains are contributing to the cave-in. Ashville has a history of this problem since the days of the Great Depression, when local householders mined their back yards for gold. Chief Wells says the intersection will be closed for the indefinite future."

"That's amazing," Nick said. "I thought all those old mines had been plugged up."

"They missed one," Julie said, with emphasis.

"I remember those mines," Mrs. Prescott said, brightening. "My grandfather said he got his family through the hard times by digging in his back yard, and when he was done, he built a garage with a basement. He was sure proud of that garage, at least until the floor collapsed and his new Ford fell through."

She appeared to be just getting started on a long story when Mr. Pitt threw down his napkin and marched out of the room. Susan followed and, soon after, Julie excused herself. Nick was next, so finally just GrandAnn and I were left listening to Mrs. Prescott.

". . . so that's how my great-uncle got into the grocery business and how his wife ran for the city council. During the war, she became our first female mayor . . ."

I tucked my new book under my arm and waved to GrandAnn. I was partway up the first flight of stairs when I heard Mrs. Prescott interrupt her own story.

"Say, Ann," she said, "didn't you leave that key on the counter? It's gone."

Chapter 11

I nestled in the window seat with Orenthal. His eyes were closed, and his chin rested on his left front paw. On my lap was a small book with violets on the cover, to match my room. Its pages were blank. Mom had given it to me.

"It's a journal," she had said. "It's for your personal thoughts and feelings. Sometimes a journal helps me think."

Until then, most of my personal thoughts and feelings weren't worthy of such a pretty book. I would have had to put down how much I hated to have my parents so far away, and that seemed selfish, so I just didn't write anything.

Now, though, I had something private and important to think about. I chatted with Orenthal while I started a list titled "Mysterious Occurrences." If I put down everything I could about the odd events of the last few days, maybe I could make sense of them. Orenthal pretended to be sleeping, but now and then his ears gave him away. They twitched. I knew he was listening.

First I wrote "Mrs. Prescott." I couldn't accept that she had been knocked out by accident. I had heard someone. I wrote "footsteps!!!"

Also, the bust of Mark Twain hadn't been high enough to fall on her head. So, who had hit her and, even more important, why? I wrote that, too. Maybe she had seen something, or someone. I put a question mark beside her name.

Next I wrote "The Portrait." Who had been in the attic that night? Whoever it was almost certainly took the Mark Twain letters. I listed the boarders, then crossed out Mr. Pitt, remembering that I had heard him playing his violin when I found the fallen picture. Any of the others could have done it by sneaking up the back stairs without being seen, except by Orenthal.

"I wish you could talk," I told him.

His ears twitched.

"I also wish I knew how you got locked in the shed," I said, and they twitched again.

Thinking of the shed brought me back to Mr. Pitt's strange behavior. I gave him a section of his own on my list. He took apples from the root cellar, but he had said at dinner that he preferred not to eat apples. He objected to the police's presence even more than Nick had, and when Mrs. Prescott started talking about the old days in Ashville, he was the first one out of the room. He was about her age; I would have thought he'd be more interested than the rest of us.

Beneath his name I wrote "shed/apples," "avoids Mrs. Prescott," and "police!" I had to admit, it looked pretty silly.

I thought about making a category for the shed,

but I wasn't sure how much of the eerie tapping and the disappearance of the padlock was the work of my vivid imagination and how much was truly mysterious and spooky.

Instead, I wrote down the names of the other three boarders. I reluctantly wrote "police record" beneath Nick's name, but couldn't think of anything to write beneath Julie's.

Below Susan's name I wrote "likes Mark Twain/ hates cats." That gave me some satisfaction, but when I read the words on the paper, they looked pretty silly, too.

Finally I wrote "The Key." Which one had taken it? It must have been one of the four, unless Mrs. Prescott just pretended to discover that it was missing and took it herself. Frustrated, I put down the pen and ran my index finger along the bottom of Orenthal's chin. He squeezed his eyes tight and sighed a rumbling purr.

It made no sense. As GrandAnn sometimes said, the only way from here to there is the letter *t*. The only thing I knew for sure was that I didn't know enough. Every time I thought I had figured out one layer of the mystery, I uncovered another layer.

"It's like peeling an onion," I said aloud. "It's a mystery wrapped in a riddle."

Still, if anyone was going to unwrap the mystery and find the thief and the letters, it looked as if it would have to be me. GrandAnn trusted everyone too much. Now that I was starting to make friends, at least I might not have to investigate alone.

I dialed Georgette's number. She answered after the third ring.

"Georgette, do you want to play detective?"

We planned it for the next day. We would come right home from school. While everyone was out, we would search the house. I wanted to start with Susan's room.

"I'm not sure we should actually go into her room," Georgette said softly. "Isn't there some kind of a law about that?"

"I have to do this," I told her. "No one else is doing anything. You don't have to help, but if you do, it will be a lot easier and safer. Think of it as doing something for GrandAnn. She deserves our help. She takes in all kinds of strays and gives people anything she has, then they take advantage of her."

That convinced Georgette.

Our first stop the next afternoon was the cleaning supply closet, where I picked up the ring of room keys. I led the way as we crept down the hall to the door of Tom Sawyer. I knocked, in case Susan was in, but there was no response. I tried the doorknob. It didn't budge. I selected the key marked *Tom* and slid it quietly into the lock. Georgette hovered beside me, looking nervously up and down the hall.

"Hurry," she whispered.

The door opened, and I stepped in. Susan's room was a mess. Crooked towers of books rose from the floor around her desk. On the desk top was a tangle of antique-style pens and bottles of ink. Drawers stood open, and a wastebasket overflowed onto the braided rug at the foot of her bed.

T-shirts, jeans, sweaters, and shoes littered the floor. I almost tripped over a pair of heavy hiking boots. The memory of those loud footsteps going down the back stairs came back to me. It could have been Susan.

"Wow, where do we start?" I said to Georgette.

The door slammed.

Startled, I turned around. Georgette was gone, but I heard her voice from beyond the door.

"Hello, Mr. Pitt," she said loudly. "You're home early."

I couldn't hear his reply, but footsteps along the hall indicated he was going to his room. I pressed my ear against the door, but no further sounds came. Then Mr. Pitt's violin started its familiar series of exercises.

"Georgette," I whispered as loudly as I dared.

Footsteps approached the door.

"Georgette," I said as I opened the door, relieved to have her back.

Susan stood there.

"Miranda, I told you not to snoop in the tenants' rooms. Susan has every right to be angry."

GrandAnn stood before me with her hands on her hips. She pressed her lips together firmly between statements. Her eyes narrowed and glittered.

I had never seen her truly furious before.

Susan sat across the kitchen table from me. Georgette had been sent home.

"Did she take anything?" Susan asked, with a nasty sneer.

"Of course not," I replied. "I only went in to . . . well, I thought . . . since you like Mark Twain so much . . ."

I took a deep breath and said it out loud. "I was looking for GrandAnn's letters. I think you took them."

The accusation sounded harsh and bold, but I wasn't sorry. Even if she had loved cats and hated peanut butter and sardines, she would still have been the most likely suspect.

"Ann, I won't put up with any more of this," Susan said. "I could cause a lot of trouble for you. Your granddaughter burglarized my room, and I hold you responsible."

"I'm sorry, Susan. You're right. She won't do anything like that again."

It hurt to hear GrandAnn apologize, especially to Susan.

"Be sure she doesn't," Susan said, with a lingering glare in my direction, then she strode out of the room.

That evening was miserable. GrandAnn didn't say any more about my entering Susan's room. She didn't say much about anything. I went to my room early. I read my book, but even when Hank Morgan confronted the wicked sorceress, Morgan Le Fay, I couldn't stay interested. Finally I slept.

Chapter 12

"My dad said he'd drive us since it's still raining."

I was relieved when Georgette called the next morning. I didn't mind walking in the rain, but I was afraid she wouldn't want to have anything to do with me. My brief career as a detective had come to an embarrassing end.

We couldn't talk on the way to school. It wasn't just that we had company; it was almost impossible to hear. The old station wagon was noisy enough, but Georgette's two younger brothers and her baby sister boosted the level from simple noise to pandemonium.

When we arrived at school, Georgette kissed her little sister and waved at her dad and brothers. Then she turned to me.

"Miranda, I'm so sorry about yesterday afternoon. I didn't know what else to do. When I heard the footsteps, I closed Susan's door. It was Mr. Pitt. He sort of stared at me, as if he thought I was up to something . . . which, of course, I was. So I went down to the living room . . . I mean Becky . . ."

She smiled shyly. "Then Susan came in and dashed up the stairs before I could do anything to warn you."

"It was a lousy idea anyway," I said, simply glad that Georgette didn't think I was a total dingbat.

"What was a lousy idea?"

It was Jess, with Tiff.

We explained how we had tried to play detective and how I had made a total fool out of myself and embarrassed my grandmother. Actually, I did the explaining. Georgette provided a sympathetic back-up.

"You did what you thought you had to do," she insisted.

"I was what GrandAnn would call a 'defective detective,' " I said.

Jess smiled, but she looked thoughtful. After a while she asked a question.

"Don't you clean the rooms sometimes?"

"Yes, once a week we vacuum. At least Mrs. Prescott does."

"Maybe she could use some help."

That is how I wound up volunteering to take Mrs. Prescott's place on Saturday morning. She had to be at a rehearsal for her melodrama, and she looked grateful when I offered to help.

GrandAnn regarded me seriously for a moment. "You have enough sense to leave things alone, don't you, Miranda?"

I assured her that I did. I wouldn't touch a thing except to vacuum the floors and dust. I meant it, too. Nothing could keep me from using my eyes, though, and I intended to use them well.

Later, armed with the vacuum and dust rags, I knocked on The Connecticut Yankee and waited for Nick's reply. There was no answer.

"It's Miranda," I called out, and let myself in with the *Yankee* key.

Nick's room was already pretty clean. All his clothes were hung up or put away in drawers. A book titled *Gold Rush and Beyond* weighed down a stack of papers. I wasn't expecting to find anything odd, anyway. I just vacuumed, dusted, and let myself out.

Mr. Pitt's room across the hall was next. It was tidy, too. A music stand stood in the corner near the window overlooking the back yard. Remembering my vow to use my eyes well, I read the title of the music: Concerto in A Minor. Beside the music stand was a table holding more sheet music in a neat stack and a small tape recorder.

His shoes were lined up on his closet floor. One pair was coated with mud, and it took me a while to get the dried mud off the carpet. He had a big metal trunk at the foot of his bed, but it was closed, and I didn't dare look into it.

On his desk was a bundle of keys. When I picked them up to dust the desk top, the key on top caught my eye. It was old-fashioned, with carving on the top. I studied the design for a second, admiring the elaborate curlicues; then I noticed that the next key looked familiar. It had a number, a palindrome.

It was 2112!

I carefully put the keys back. Checking the room

to be sure it looked as though nothing had been disturbed, I vacuumed my way out the door, backward.

"Hi, Miranda."

Julie's voice startled me. She seemed not to notice my nervousness. She chatted as she led the way to her room and swung the door wide.

"I was expecting Mrs. Prescott."

The Huck Finn Room has a window facing the side yard, but the view to the back is blocked by the chimney rising from the fireplace below. Once this room also had a fireplace, but it was bricked over years ago. An old quilt hangs like a painting against the bricks.

Julie set up an ironing board beside the window and busied herself with a pile of blouses. The roar of the vacuum prevented conversation, so we worked without talking.

The old, unused hearth had a few bits of crumbled stone scattered across it. I turned off the vacuum and bent to brush the lose grit off the hearth, then stood there a moment, admiring the quilt.

Tiny stitches marched across the colored fabric, tracing an intricate design. It was hard to imagine the patience of the stitcher. Endless hours of delicate, repetitive work went into each quilt. GrandAnn had told me that before they were married, girls used to make many quilts to warm their future families. Someone my age might have created this one.

The quilt was beautiful, but I was glad I had the choice of using an electric blanket.

77

As I turned to mention that thought to Julie, the long handle of the upright vacuum hit the quilt. It scraped across the brickwork. I heard a rustle and a soft, sighing sound behind me.

"Oh my gosh!" Julie exclaimed.

There on the hearth, bound with a blue ribbon, lay a bundle of letters.

Chapter 13

"I can't imagine how they got there."

Julie sounded truly bewildered as she handed the letters to GrandAnn.

"Oh, Julie, this is wonderful!"

GrandAnn reached for the letters tenderly, as if they were a newly hatched chick or a pink rosebud, and said, "It doesn't matter how they were found. The important thing is that they are here. Thank you."

Orenthal wove himself in figure eights between Julie's and GrandAnn's legs, purring.

GrandAnn called Officer Carlson to tell him the good news. Within five minutes he was at the door, hat in hand. I think he was almost as happy as we were to have the letters back, but he wanted to question Julie more carefully than GrandAnn had.

"They're back. That's all that matters," GrandAnn insisted.

"The fact remains that the letters were stolen. I'd feel a lot better if we knew who did it."

All Julie could tell us was that she was as surprised as I was when the letters fell from their hiding place. I had to admit that she did seem surprised.

"Someone could have put them in your room," I

offered. "All they would have had to do was get the key from the cleaning closet."

We left it at that. GrandAnn wouldn't have believed Julie had taken the letters anyway.

"What matters is that they're back," she repeated. She gently opened each envelope and laid the letters out on the kitchen table. We gathered around to watch.

"The first letter is missing because it's in San Francisco," GrandAnn explained. "I sent it there to have it examined, to be sure Mark Twain really wrote it. The rest are in order, here.

"The one in San Francisco was dated 1865. It mentions his story about the jumping frog. Here is the next one, dated 1866. It was sent from Hawaii. Then there is one from the year his first book of short stories came out, 1867, and two from 1869. The last three aren't dated."

She straightened up and sighed deeply. "They're all here except the one I sent away. Thunder, I'm glad to have them back."

GrandAnn placed the letters gently on the kitchen table and asked us not to touch them. We bent over the table, our hands clasped behind our backs to avoid the temptation to caress the fragile pages.

The paper was yellowed and the ink was faded in places, but once I got used to the old-fashioned script, I found myself enjoying what Mark Twain had written. They weren't love letters. Part of me was sorry and part was relieved. I could imagine my great-great-grandmother as a girl, and later as a young woman, living in this remote village in Oregon and seeing the world through his eyes. No wonder she treasured his letters.

Julie must have felt it, too. I heard her catch her breath now and then, and once she actually giggled. Her reaction seemed so natural that I was even more sure this was the first time she had read them.

I was amused to discover why GrandAnn says "Thunder!" Mark Twain used that expression in the second letter. He called my great-great-grandmother "Miss Anne" and spoke often about how much he had enjoyed his "sojourn West." In the letter written in 1866, he told the story of how Yreka got its name.

He said the town was brand new and needed a name badly. The local baker had painted a canvas sign to advertise his business and had put it out to dry in the sun. A stranger rode into town and saw the sign. It was facing the opposite direction, so the stranger saw it backward. But because the sun was behind it, he could read the letters plainly. The *B* was blocked by the side of the building, and all the stranger could make out was YREKA. He called the town Yreka, and the local miners agreed that the name was as good as any. It stuck.

No wonder my grandmother liked Mark Twain. He was a riddler, too.

Officer Carlson read the letters with us. He chuckled now and then, and he was grinning when he finished, but then he sat down and spoke to GrandAnn seriously.

81

"Ma'am, I still think you should be very careful. You don't know who took the letters."

"I'm certain it wasn't Julie," GrandAnn replied stubbornly, and I agreed with her.

"Maybe not, but there's a good possibility that someone attacked your housekeeper. It looks like someone capable of violence wanted those letters and probably still wants them. I think you have a thief in your house, a dangerous thief."

GrandAnn responded by gathering the letters, wrapping them carefully in a clean dishtowel, and picking up her purse.

"I'll take them to the safe deposit box right now," she declared.

"Good," he said. "Please let me take you there, just to be on the safe side."

They left together. The bounce in GrandAnn's stride told me clearly that she, at least, was satisfied.

I was still troubled, though. When the officer talked about the thief being violent, another idea had struck me. What if the thief and the attacker weren't the same person? I was puzzling over this new riddle when Julie interrupted.

"What did he mean when he said someone attacked your housekeeper? Was Mrs. Prescott hurt?"

I told her about hearing a struggle and finding Mrs. Prescott on the landing.

"I'm sure someone hit her on the head, but she claims no one was with her," I said. "How could she be hit from the front and not know who did it?"

"She wouldn't remember," Julie said with certainty. "One of my professors was explaining that just last week. When a person is hit on the head hard enough to be knocked unconscious, the memory of what happened is always missing. Amnesia is one of the signs of concussion. She wouldn't be able to remember someone hitting her, even if she tried."

"So there was someone," I said.

I felt better and worse at the same time: worse because now I was certain someone had been there, and better because at least I didn't doubt myself anymore. It hadn't been my imagination.

"Thanks, Julie."

She hugged me, and we went back to her room, Julie to finish her ironing and I to continue my vacuuming chores. There didn't seem to be much point in snooping in Susan's room anymore, but I had to finish the cleaning. I knocked, called out, and went in with my gear.

Susan's room was still a mess. I had to move piles of clothes and books to get at the floor. It seemed a bit fruitless to clean the floor only to cover it with junk again, but my parents had always told me to tolerate other people's styles, and we had lived in so many kinds of places that I was used to different ways of doing things.

I was thinking along those lines and feeling a little smug about being so open-minded when the vacuum hit a pile of books, and they spread out across the floor like an opened fan. The top book was larger than those beneath it, which is probably why the stack had been so wobbly. I picked it up, and a stack of letters fell out.

A word on the top page caught my eye: *Yreka*. I flipped through the pages. Phrases echoed the letters I had read just an hour ago: "Hawaii," "sojourn West," "Thunder!" and something new: "Jim Smiley and His Jumping Frog."

I could hardly believe what I was seeing. The letters in my hand looked just like the ones GrandAnn had taken with her. The creases in the paper and the paper itself seemed identical. The handwriting was similar. The only thing different was the extra letter, the one about the jumping frog.

My first impulse was to take the letters for GrandAnn, but then I remembered her stern face when she had said, "No snooping." Surely anyone who saw me there on the floor sorting through the stack of spilled books would think I was searching Susan's room.

Besides, GrandAnn had been confident that her letters were genuine. She had them in a safe place now. I decided not to do anything just yet.

I replaced the pages in the big book, restacked the pile, and was backing out the door when Susan came up behind me.

"Just finishing," I said.

"Thanks," she muttered ungraciously, and pushed through into her room. The door slammed behind her.

Chapter 14

I rushed up to my room and called Georgette, then Tiff, then Jess. I needed to figure out what to do about the letters in Susan's room, and about the key which, apparently, Mr. Pitt had lost in the root cellar.

It felt good to have someone to talk with. It felt wonderful, but I was too worried to enjoy it much. The girls agreed to meet me at the movie theater that afternoon, and they each sounded eager to help.

I needed to talk with someone other than GrandAnn. I didn't think she would be able to believe that I had found the letters in Susan's room by accident. I wasn't even sure it mattered. Didn't GrandAnn have the original letters safe in the bank? I wished I could be sure.

By the time Georgette came by for me, the rain had stopped, although the sun was still muted by high clouds. We wore sweaters and jackets to fight the chill.

"I'm glad you could come," I said. "I just can't figure out what to do. It helps to have another person's ideas."

I avoided the word *friend,* not wanting to seem too anxious. I shouldn't have worried.

"That's what friends are for," Georgette said in a matter-of-fact way. "Friends are supposed to help each other." She paused until she had the right words, then said, "I know how it feels to be alone. It isn't fun."

I didn't know how to answer her, so I didn't say anything. Our silence grew, but it wasn't uncomfortable.

This is what friends are for, I thought, echoing her words, silently. I matched my footsteps to hers.

Halfway down the block a car horn sounded behind us. We turned to see Jess's mom waving from their old truck. She dropped off Jess and Tiff and drove away with another cheerful wave. On the way to the theater at the center of town, I told them about the letters and the key.

"So we were right from the beginning," Jess said. "That first day we thought Susan took the letters."

"But GrandAnn has the letters," I pointed out, confused.

"It's like that book by Mark Twain, the one I got from the library last week."

The Tragedy of Pudd'nhead Wilson," I said, remembering.

"Yes. It's an odd story. A mother switches her slave baby for the son of the rich man. That's what I think Susan did: a switch."

"You mean she copied them?" I asked, remembering all the pens and different kinds of ink in the litter of Susan's room. "I'd better tell GrandAnn."

Georgette asked a question I couldn't answer. "Will you be able to explain how you found the second set?"

I remembered how angry GrandAnn had been when Susan found Georgette and me snooping upstairs.

"Maybe I should wait until Susan is out and look again," I decided. "She's usually gone on Sunday afternoons. I'll go up tomorrow and get the letters. It will be easier to explain if I have proof."

"We still have to explain the mysterious Aloysius Pitt, a.k.a. Al," Tiff said. "How did he lose his key in your root cellar?"

Georgette laughed. "He was after the apples. That must be when he dropped his key."

"But he doesn't like apples," I countered.

"Maybe they were a gift for someone," she answered, still grinning at the memory of his struggle with the heavy bag.

"Maybe," I said. "Or maybe they were just an excuse for being there."

"But why?" Jess asked.

I just shook my head. I didn't know.

"When I put one piece of the puzzle in place, another piece pops out," I said.

A noisy crowd had gathered around the barricade at the intersection of Main and Agate. We joined them to peer down into the caved-in street that had been built over a forgotten mine. It was just a hole, but a huge one, big enough to easily swallow GrandAnn's sports car.

"It's hard to believe that people were so desperate that they dug up their own yards," I said.

"I think people who are desperate will do almost anything," Georgette answered. "And, Miranda, you shouldn't be careless around Susan. If you go into her room again, be careful. She must be the one who hid the letters in Julie's room."

Suddenly I remembered Orenthal's adventure. Maybe Susan had left her door open when she went into Julie's room, and that was when Orenthal gave in to the temptation of her sardine sandwich. No wonder Susan had been so irritated.

"She might even have tried to kill Mrs. Prescott," Georgette went on. "If she would do that, she would hurt you or your grandmother, too."

Before I could digest that horrible thought, I heard Tiff start to giggle in a way that could only mean *boys*. Sure enough, Tim and Josh were crossing the street toward us. They waved, and we waved back. We got in line together, and when Steve arrived, we let him in line, too.

I tried to enjoy the movie and my new friends, but I knew Georgette was right. Something was still going on, and someone still might be hurt.

Sunday was quiet. It was the kind of day that brought out the charm in The Jumping Frog. The sun returned in full strength, intensifying the yellow of the early daffodils against the green lawn. The fireplace in Becky Thatcher held a cheerful blaze to drive out any remnants of chill. GrandAnn fixed an

88

elaborate brunch for just the two of us, with fresh cinnamon peach bread, cheese soufflé, baked apples with whipping cream, and hot spiced cider.

The rose and mauve patterned wallpaper was dappled with sun coming through the lace curtains. Orenthal chose the hearth for his postbrunch nap, and I sprawled in the huge stuffed chair and tried to concentrate on my book.

The Connecticut Yankee had installed telephones in King Arthur's court and was impressing the knights of the Round Table with his "magic." I wished I had some magic, real or otherwise, to help me get those letters out of Susan's room. My mind drifted in and out of the novel, but it felt good being there with GrandAnn and Orenthal. It felt like family in an easy way.

GrandAnn was taking a rare moment to relax with a book, but hers was about teaching adults to read.

"It's for the literacy project. We have to include parents, as well as the children."

She sighed. "I'm so glad the trouble about those letters is finished. Now we can get on with just being a family."

She often seemed to know what I was thinking, but this was so close I had to laugh aloud.

She was right. Once I pushed nagging questions about the letters and the root cellar aside, the future did seem clear. I would finish the year in a new school with new friends. In three months my folks would come home, for good this time. Next summer GrandAnn and I would help migrant workers learn how to read. Next fall I would start a second year in the same school!

"What's a six-letter word that means something you put on shoes in lower case, and some people in the news in upper case?" GrandAnn had turned her attention to the Sunday crossword puzzle. I was still trying to grasp her question when the phone rang.

GrandAnn answered it with a bright "Hello! This is The Jumping Frog. How may I help you?"

She listened to the caller intently, and I could see the brightness fade from her face. Tension crept into her posture, and I could hear it in her voice. Quietly, she thanked the caller and placed the receiver in its cradle.

"GrandAnn, what's wrong?"

"That was the document examiner. She says the Twain letter is a forgery."

Her shoulders dropped as she sat on the edge of the couch, and she shook her head ruefully. "Such a fuss, and the letters were fakes all along. I should have known they couldn't be real. I wanted to believe in them so much, I guess I fooled myself."

"GrandAnn," I said, "there's something I have to tell you."

When I told her about cleaning Susan's room and spilling the pile of books, she didn't even look skeptical. I should have known she would believe me.

"I think Susan switched copies for your letters. One of the letters in her room mentioned the jumping frog story. I think she has the whole set."

GrandAnn frowned and nodded slowly. "She was

here the day we found them," she said. "She must have started to make copies right away, replacing my letters with forgeries. By the time I sent the first letter away, she had already copied it. I'll bet she was trying to put the finished copies back behind the portrait when it fell. You and Orenthal scared her off."

"I think Orenthal scared her," I said. "If she saw a cat in the attic, she might have dropped the picture trying to get out of there."

Orenthal's ears twitched at the sound of his name. He rolled over onto his back and reached as far as he could with his front legs, then his back legs.

"I think you must be right about Susan's hiding the letters in Julie's room," GrandAnn went on. "If they were found there, poor Julie would be blamed."

"And that's also probably how Orenthal got into Susan's room." I was eager to explain my theory. "Susan left the door open while she was hiding the forged letters across the hall. Orenthal just gave in to his yearning for sardines."

Orenthal trembled.

"I think the cruelest part is that I would always have thought my letters were fakes," GrandAnn said softly. "I would have thought that my grandmother made up the whole thing."

I couldn't help adding one more barb. "Susan must have been laughing at us."

GrandAnn rose from the couch and strode to the stairs. "I'll talk to her right now," she said with determination. "I want my letters back."

She looked ten feet tall as she marched up the stairs. Orenthal and I followed her at a respectful distance. We hadn't quite reached the second-floor hallway when GrandAnn cried out.

"Thunder! She's gone."

Julie came out of her room and looked over GrandAnn's shoulder. Orenthal and I came up from behind. Nick stuck his head out of his door down the hall. Mr. Pitt didn't appear, but his violin continued its constant song.

Sure enough, the room was empty. Books, clothes, pens, and papers — all were gone.

"She left last night," Nick offered. He was in his stocking feet and held a shoe in one hand and a rag in the other. "I helped her move her boxes down the stairs."

He looked surprised. "Didn't you know she was leaving?"

GrandAnn shook her head. "I don't know exactly how he's going to take it, but I think I have to call Officer Carlson again."

We waited for Officer Carlson in Becky Thatcher. I was relieved that I didn't have to sneak back into Susan's room for the letters, but annoyed with myself for leaving them there the day before. Then I remembered my other discovery.

"GrandAnn, I saw the key again."

She tilted her chin up and listened while I explained seeing the key with the palindrome on Mr. Pitt's desk.

"Well," she said at last, "we know now he is guilty

of being in the root cellar. Miranda, we already knew that."

Her voice softened, and I could tell she was trying to be gentle with me. But she sounded a little impatient when she added, "I hope you can learn not to distrust someone just because you don't like his manner. We owe people the benefit of a doubt. You don't have to like everyone, but you should try to believe that each person does his or her best in life. It isn't up to you to judge."

"I was right about Susan," I said. I couldn't help defending myself.

"We still don't know the final story, even about her," GrandAnn replied firmly and picked up her crossword puzzle again.

I opened my book. There didn't seem to be anything more to say. Something tickled at my mind, though: the image of Nick and his shiny black shoe. Then it came to me.

"I've got it," I said. "Something you put on shoes is polish."

GrandAnn finished it for me, her good humor slipping back in place. "Some people in the news are Polish."

She was penciling in the letters when the doorbell rang. It was Officer Carlson.

Chapter 15

GrandAnn sat on the edge of the big sofa in the Becky Thatcher Room. Finding the letters, or thinking she had, then losing them again had taken something out of her. She seemed more tiny and more fragile than ever.

She hadn't stopped trusting, though, or making excuses for people. I had just listened to her spend fifteen minutes trying to convince the officer that she was partly to blame for Susan's dishonesty.

"Susan is young. It was wrong of me to tempt her with the letters. I knew she was a fanatic about Mark Twain. She probably thought she wasn't doing any real harm, as long as I believed my copies were genuine. Once we find her, she'll see that what she did was wrong, and she'll be glad to return the letters."

GrandAnn twisted her hands together in her lap as she talked. I wanted to do something. Or hit something. Or someone. Instead, I tried to be inconspicuous. I listened and watched, and vowed silently to do everything I could to make sure GrandAnn's letters were returned.

Officer Carlson tried to be encouraging, but at the end he told GrandAnn that he had little hope of finding Susan or the letters.

94

"She knows we're looking for her by now, and she knows she has committed a serious crime. Also, she has had a day's head start. We'll have a hard time finding her."

Georgette was full of questions when she came by for me on Monday morning.

"How did it go? Did you get the letters back?"

"It's worse than ever," I said, then explained about Susan's disappearance. "It turns out she was already gone when I got home from the movies Saturday night."

As we walked to school, Georgette and I talked about ways to find Susan, but we hadn't figured out any brilliant ideas by the time we got there. Jess and Tiff were already on the playground, standing with Jess's cousin, Corky.

Corky is a cute little kid with red hair. He had a football in the crook of one arm and a grin the size of a football field. When we joined them, he said hi, waved at Georgette, and headed down the block toward John Ball Elementary School.

"We want to do an article for the school paper on the cave-in downtown," Jess said.

Tiff indicated her camera, perched on top of the stack of books she clutched close to her chest. "I want to get a shot of it before they start to fill it in. Wouldn't it be weird to be standing on the street and to have it just . . . *swoosh* . . . disappear?"

Her eyes brightened at the idea.

"Let's go together after school," I said, thinking

about Susan when Tiff said "just . . . *swoosh* . . . disappear." "I need your help more than ever."

"Can Corky come along? I have to take care of him after school today," Jess asked.

"Sure. Maybe he'll see something we miss," I said.

After school the five of us walked up the street, more or less together. Corky tossed his football, rushed to catch it, then stopped to toss it again. A series of jerky dashes carried him up the sidewalk.

"Isn't football season over?" I asked.

Jess smiled a little. "For Corky, it is always football season," she answered.

Tiff stopped every time she saw an odd crack in the pavement or a leafless tree tracing a crack against the sky.

"Picturesque," she would mutter, and look through the camera to frame an imaginary shot. Sometimes she actually took a picture.

We were in no hurry. Even Georgette had the afternoon off from baby-sitting. We stayed with Tiff each time she stopped to fuss over a winterkilled marigold or a budding crocus.

When we reached the intersection, Tiff walked all around the barricade, studying it from every angle. Then she chose three sites and took her pictures. Jess found a worker who was glad to stop and answer questions. Corky sifted through a pile of dirt that had been dumped beside the hole. He said he was searching for gold.

Georgette and I enjoyed the bustle from the

sidelines. I must have jumped when I saw Mr. Pitt, because Georgette gave me a startled glance, then turned to see what I was looking at. Together we watched Mr. Pitt's slightly stooped figure approach from the direction of The Bard's Theater. I thought he was going to ignore us, but when I said hello, he grunted and clutched his violin case tighter. Then, surprising me, he stopped beside us and gazed into the shallow crater.

"Gold," he said. "All that gold; all that hard work. It's gone, now. They worked their lives away and all that's left is an empty pit."

His face wrinkled, and he made a coughing, wheezing sound.

Before he walked off toward The Jumping Frog, he repeated, "An empty pit."

That was the only time I ever heard Mr. Pitt laugh.

Tiff was just finishing taking her pictures when Nick joined us. "Hi, Miranda. Introduce me to your friends."

I did. Georgette ducked her head and smiled at Nick. Jess held out her hand, and he shook it. Tiff giggled a little, but managed to actually start a conversation as we all walked together toward The Jumping Frog.

"Why did they tunnel in their own back yards?" she asked.

Nick answered with enthusiasm. While he talked, I remembered seeing the book about gold mining in his room.

"I've been reading about that. They were poor. It was the time of the Great Depression. People dug buckets of dirt and gravel out of their back yards. They didn't find anything as big as a nugget. They were after the gold dust mingled with the dirt. They washed the dirt down big wooden troughs, called sluice boxes, and the heavy gold dust settled out. They might have made enough to feed their families, but I don't think many of them got rich. It was hard work. They eventually filled in the holes and went on with life. Almost any other kind of job is easier than that kind of gold mining."

Jess took notes while he talked and made sure she had his name spelled right for her article.

GrandAnn and Mrs. Prescott were in the kitchen playing checkers when we got to The Jumping Frog. GrandAnn jumped up and insisted on fixing hot chocolate for everyone. We didn't try to discourage her.

Mrs. Prescott told Jess the story of her grandfather's mine and the collapsed garage floor, while Jess took more notes for her article.

"Do you actually remember the back-yard mines?" Jess asked her.

"Oh, indeed I do. I was just about your age then, just getting the hang of being a teenager."

She looked at GrandAnn and grinned. "Miranda's grandmother is a mite too young to recall it. She was still a baby, not even school age. But I used to help my grandmother cook for the hired hands, and some days I got to go along to sell the dust.

"I didn't know any better. I thought it was fun, but a lot of folks were hurting. They were seriously hungry. It wasn't fun for them."

"Some folks are hungry, even today," GrandAnn said gently as she arranged our four mugs of hot chocolate on a tray and handed a fifth mug to Corky.

As I lifted the tray to carry it upstairs, the sound of Mr. Pitt's violin came down the staircase to us.

"What's he playing?" Tiff asked.

"I know," I answered, remembering what I had seen in his room on Saturday. "It's something in A minor."

Mrs. Prescott looked puzzled, then astonished, but she didn't reply. She just sat down again at the table and studied the checkerboard with an uncharacteristic frown.

Corky stayed in the kitchen, stroking Orenthal under the chin and whispering to him. Orenthal looked as though he understood every word and devoted himself to being sure that each of Corky's fingers had an equal opportunity to reach behind his ears.

Then Corky said something that puzzled me.

He looked up at GrandAnn and commented, "You must like football a lot."

"Why yes," she answered, sounding surprised and delighted. "Yes, as a matter of fact, I do."

I led the way upstairs and stopped to rest the heavy tray against the banister on the second-floor landing. My friends clustered around the doorway, peering into the empty hallway. None of the borders were in sight, but violin music flooded out from Mr. Pitt's room.

Then Tiff did something outrageous. She leaned forward into the hallway and looked around with jerky little head movements and wide-open eyes, like an actor in an old silent movie. With a finger pressed tightly to her lips, she crept down the hallway on tiptoe. She stopped at the room marked Pudd'n-head Wilson, rolled her eyes, and pressed her ear against the door.

GrandAnn is almost fanatic about her boarders' privacy and I was in enough trouble already, so I stayed with Georgette on the landing. But Tiff's elaborate pantomime was hard to resist. I was afraid Mr. Pitt might hear us, but I couldn't stop myself from giggling. I heard Georgette behind me. She was giggling, too.

Jess almost choked on a burst of laughter, and she rushed to tug at Tiff's arm. "Come on, Tiff," she coaxed in a kind of whispered shout. "If he comes out, *you'll* be the pudd'nhead."

Tiff was convinced. She and Jess scooted back to the safety of the stairwell.

"What if he had caught you there?" Georgette asked as we climbed up to the third floor.

"I had a plan," Tiff answered. "As soon as the

music stopped, I would have run. He'd never catch me."

Tiff exclaimed over my room. She called the walls "lilac" and the white bedspread "alabaster." Jess giggled and said that Tiff had three names for every color in, or out of, the rainbow. Georgette perched on the window seat and balanced her hot chocolate on her knee. Tiff sat beside her. Jess sat at my desk, and I took the floor.

"It looks like you were right," I told Jess. "Susan copied the letters and switched them. The ones I found in Julie's room were fakes. Now we have to find Susan to get the real letters back."

Tiff looked disappointed. "I thought it was the violinist. He was the perfect villain," she said. "I was sure he was the one who beat up on poor old Mrs. Prescott."

She said it with such relish I had to smile.

"It did sound like a man's footsteps," I said, "and he's certainly grumpy enough to be scary sometimes. I just don't know why he would attack her. At least Susan might have had a motive. Maybe Mrs. Prescott had found something incriminating in her room. But we can't ask her until we find her."

"Maybe she found something incriminating in Mr. Pitt's room," Jess said.

That gave me something to think about.

"Why not put an ad in the paper?" Georgette suggested, changing the subject back to Susan. "Offer some kind of reward for the letters."

"Or a personal ad," Jess said, catching Georgette's train of thought. "Tell Susan she won't be in trouble if she returns them."

"GrandAnn would like both of those ideas," I said.

Tiff had been gazing out the window. "Oh, how beautiful," she said. "Just look at the color of those daffodils in the afternoon light!"

She tilted her head from side to side, studying the view, then she picked up her camera. Kneeling on the window seat, she snapped a picture. "I'll have a copy made for you," she said.

We finished our chocolate and carried the cups back to the kitchen, with no stops on the second floor this time. GrandAnn listened politely to our ideas and thanked us.

"I'll be sure to pass them on to Officer Carlson," she said. "I really do thank you for being concerned about my loss, girls. It's nice to know that you care so much."

"One other thing, GrandAnn. We were wondering if The Jumping Frog has any other secret passages or hiding places, like the one in the chimney."

Her eyes flashed with sudden amusement, like a child's. "Wouldn't that be exciting? Sliding panels, you mean, or tunnels or cavities in the walls?" Then she shook her head with regret and said, "My grandfather always claimed he had a hidden mine, but that must have been up in the hills, if it ever existed. I'm afraid we'll have to make do with present mysteries."

Jess and Corky were on their way out when I

thought to ask Corky how he knew GrandAnn liked football.

"That's easy," he said. "She named her cat Orenthal. The only other Orenthal I know of is one of the best football players in history, O. J. Simpson. O. J. stands for Orenthal James."

"I would never have figured that one out myself," I told Jess. "Didn't I say Corky might see something we missed?"

Later, alone, I sat in the window seat and thought about GrandAnn's letters. A week ago, I didn't know they existed. Then they were lost, then found, then lost again, this time along with Susan.

I felt disgusted with myself for leaving them in her room, but at the time it had seemed like the best thing to do. It was my responsibility to help get them back, but everything I tried or suggested was brushed aside, as if I had nothing important to contribute.

Even with my new friends, I felt more alone than ever. I wished I had Mom and Dad to talk to. I flopped on my bed and lay there, thinking, as the sunlight faded.

Finally I tired of feeling sorry for myself, having what my dad would have called a "pity party." The thought of him made me smile, and I went to my desk to start a letter. Maybe writing everything to my folks would help me figure out what to do next. I reached for the switch on my desk lamp when a flicker of light from the alley stopped me.

Probably a headlight reflecting off the shed, I thought.

I knelt on the window seat for a closer look. That wasn't a car. A thin, steady shaft of light streamed across the grass. The light came from inside the shed.

Chapter 16

I rattled down the stairs, passed the empty hallway on the second floor, and landed in the kitchen. GrandAnn stood by the stove, softly humming the tune that Mr. Pitt was playing upstairs.

"There's someone in the shed," I told her breathlessly. "Maybe it's Susan."

"Thunder," GrandAnn said, "what on earth would she be doing out there?"

She wiped her hands on a dishtowel and stepped through the swinging door into Becky Thatcher. A moment later she was back with a sweater and my old windbreaker. I flicked on the porch light and squinted out into the back yard. A shadow shifted in the alley, but nothing more. The light from the shed had gone out. I picked the lightning bug flashlight out of GrandAnn's tool drawer and followed her as she hurried down the path to the shed.

I didn't know what to expect, but it certainly was not what we found. The door was firmly shut, and the padlock hung in place. GrandAnn slipped the lock off the latch, opened the door, and peered in. I sent the beam of the flashlight into the corners. Shelves and shadows greeted us, nothing else.

"Is anyone there?" GrandAnn called out.

Of course there was no answer.

She replaced the lock and led the way back to the kitchen. I tried not to look at her.

"False alarm," she said lightly, but I knew what she was thinking: more imaginary gremlins.

Mr. Pitt stood in the kitchen, pouring himself a cup of coffee. He didn't take much notice of our breathless arrival. He nodded curtly to us, but he didn't say a word. He took his coffee and marched back up to his room.

I flopped in a chair and gazed down at the flashlight I still held tightly in my hands. I turned it over and over, studying the lightning bug on the side. It was easier than meeting GrandAnn's eyes.

When she finally spoke, it was with a faraway voice, as if she were coming back from a trip into her own past. She was still looking at the stairway where Mr. Pitt had disappeared.

"I agree with Mrs. Prescott. I feel as though I know him. He reminds me a little of someone I used to know, someone Nick's age."

I stayed and tried to make small talk with GrandAnn, but I kept thinking about that padlock. I was sure that when we arrived at the shed door it had been swinging, as if someone had just put it there.

The lightning bug on the flashlight had reminded me of a joke Dad used to make the summer we spent in Iowa, where lightning bugs danced every evening.

106

"Do you know how to make a glowworm happy, GrandAnn?"

"I'm afraid not," she said, trying to be helpful.

"Dip its tail in black ink. It will be de-lighted."

She rewarded me with a smile. I agreed, it didn't deserve an actual laugh. Then she rewarded me again.

"You sound a lot like your father," she said.

The next day Tiff and Jess were watching for us when we arrived at school. Tiff positively vibrated with excitement.

"I went to the one-hour photo shop yesterday," she said. "I needed the shots of the cave-in."

She bit her lip and bounced on her feet as if her shoes had miniature trampolines inside them. With a triumphant grin she thrust a stack of pictures toward me. "Take a look at this!"

I stared at the top photograph. Tiff had captured the bright yellow daffodils. The walk, with its yellow border, wove a strand of silver across the back yard. The shed stood gray and angular at the end of the walk.

"Don't you see?" she asked. "There by the shed."

I looked more closely. A figure stood half concealed by the side of the shed. It was Mr. Pitt.

"It's just Aloysius," I said wickedly. "He lurks around the root cellar and plots to rid us of apples so GrandAnn can't make any more pies. He's a secret apple hater."

Jess interrupted my sarcasm by dropping a bomb.

"It's like in the book. You think someone is somewhere, but he's really somewhere else. In *Pudd'n-head Wilson*, it's because he's twins, or because he is someone else, because his mother exchanged him . . ."

She faltered, seeing my confused expression. Then she took a breath and started again, more slowly.

"He can't be two places at once, can he? When Tiff took the picture he was playing the violin in his room."

When I got home from school that afternoon, I opened the journal Mom had given me. On the page marked "Mysterious Occurrences," I crossed out Nick, Julie, and Mrs. Prescott as suspects. I put a huge red question mark beside Susan's name and wrote "where?"

Then I moved down to the part marked "The Key." If I ignored Susan and the letters, everything centered around the root cellar and mostly involved Mr. Pitt, the man who could seem to be in two places at once. I felt certain I had that figured out. He had used his tape recorder to make us think he was in his room. Practice pieces are played over and over again, so we wouldn't think the repetition was odd. Mrs. Prescott may have figured it out, too, when she was cleaning his room. Maybe she had gone in when the tape was on, but he wasn't there. Or maybe she figured out who he really was.

I shivered when I realized that he might have

actually been trying to kill her. He couldn't count on her losing her memory. He must have been relieved when she didn't remember the blow or what she had seen just before he hit her.

So what was he doing during all those hours when we thought he was in his room? I didn't have an answer, but I knew the best place to start would be the root cellar. I might even find the letters there.

I updated my journal. Mom had been right. It did help me think. Then I carried the journal into the storage area and ran my fingers across the bricks. When I found the smooth one, I slid it aside and slipped the book into the secret chamber, then replaced the brick.

I thought of asking Georgette to help me, but I didn't want to get her into trouble again. Besides, it was because of my carelessness that the letters were gone. I could only make up for the mistake by helping GrandAnn myself.

I changed into old jeans, then put on a pair of long socks and rolled them up over my pant legs. A wooly green sweater was next, and a windbreaker with tight cuffs and a drawstring on the collar. I pulled it snug against my neck. Then I found a knitted hat and pulled it down over my forehead and ears.

I looked in the mirror.

Silly looking, but spiderproof, I thought.

On the way through the kitchen I grabbed the flashlight. I was ready except for one thing.

I left the note anchored by the blue bowl. Once again it was full of red apples.

> GrandAnn, dear,
>
> The fruits of your labor and of the field call. I'm off to seek the thread that binds us. Don't despair. I'll be back before dinner.
>
> > Love you,
> > Miranda
>
> P.S. I'm going to shed some light on our riddle.
> P.P.S. For more, look in a place that warms your heart but cools your hearth.

I closed the back door behind me, took a deep breath, and set out.

The padlock was in place. I had almost expected it not to be. I unhooked it and swung the hasp open. The late afternoon light was softly bright. Thankful for that, I swung the door open and peered into the dark chamber.

Nothing looked out of place. I switched on the flashlight and ran its beam down the stairs. I edged out onto the first step and tried not to think of what might lurk in the dark space behind each riser. I started down.

After descending only three steps, I heard a rustling sound, like something soft and heavy being dragged across the floor, or maybe like a soft, heavy animal shifting in its sleep. I whirled and shined the light between the steps. Dancing shadows greeted me, nothing more solid than shadows.

"The curse of a gifted imagination," I muttered aloud, trying to evoke the lighthearted approach GrandAnn would take, but it didn't quite work.

I searched along the lower shelves with the light, looking for any clue to Mr. Pitt's interest in our root cellar. I pushed jars of Piccalilli Piquant aside, in case the letters had been slipped behind them. I scrunched up my courage and groped along the back edges where the shelves joined the wall. My fingers brushed against sticky cobwebs, but nothing else.

Next I moved the baskets of apples and potatoes. Nothing.

I took all of the apples out of one basket, in case some clue might be stashed beneath them. Nothing.

I started on the next basket. This was beginning to feel less like an adventure and more like work.

My eyes had adjusted to the darkness. The light through the open door, aided by the flashlight, felt more friendly.

Cobwebs hung gracefully from the ceiling and between the shelves like crepe-paper party decorations. So far I had not seen even one spider. I started to relax, and I congratulated myself for being brave and level-headed, an unusual trait in our family.

My search began close to the stairs and covered each section of shelves on the right, then on the

111

left. Section by section, my courage grew. Farthest back, the shelves were hidden deep in gloomy shadows. Light from the door could not penetrate that far, and the daylight was fading quickly.

One section to go. I was almost at the back wall now, and I bent over to shine the light under the lowest shelf.

That sound again.

Like an animal searching the darkest corners.

Like a body being dragged across the floor.

Like a giant snake, rearranging its heavy coils.

Like . . .

The idea of gremlins and goblins didn't seem funny anymore. The idea of spiders as big as basketballs suddenly seemed very reasonable.

I shrieked.

The sound echoed in the little chamber and scared me even more. I leaped up and flashed the light across the back wall. I couldn't believe my eyes.

The weathered gray boards shifted slightly toward me, then settled back. Again they moved, as if some giant animal were behind them, trying to escape.

I shrieked again and backed away. My feet got tangled with each other, and I fell heavily backwards. The light dropped and went out. The door slammed shut behind me.

Before me, the sounds behind the wall gained intensity. In back of me, footsteps approached down the stairs.

Chapter 17

Desperate to see, I fumbled for the flashlight. I groped wildly along the shelf, knocking over a can of nails. They clattered across the floor. A jar skittered off the bottom shelf, and the shattering glass covered the sound of approaching footsteps. Finally my fingers closed over the light.

I flicked it on and twisted onto my back, holding the flashlight before me like a charm to ward off evil. The beam seemed to glide across the walls in slow motion. At last it fell on an astonished face.

Mr. Pitt!

If I hadn't been so frightened, I might have laughed. He stood at the foot of the stairs, not ten feet away from me. In his right hand he carried his violin case. I had an insane idea that he was looking for a private place to practice.

His face was a medley of emotion. It went from astonishment to alarm, from alarm to fear, and from fear to anger. Fear combined with anger is dangerous. This man no longer resembled the grumpy, slouching violinist I had made jokes about. The man before me was transformed into a vortex of rage. In some instinctive way I knew that he would hurt me.

I thought of a mouse I had seen fighting desperately against Orenthal. At the time when its fate seemed certain, a strange quiet fell over it. It watched in almost calm fascination as the cat delivered its final blow.

I felt like that: horrified but also fascinated, and strangely calm.

"Interfering brat!" Mr. Pitt spat. "Now I'll have to deal with you as well as that other nitwit."

He snapped the latch of the violin case open and drew out a gun.

I've seen it happen in the movies. It looks simple. One person holds out a gun. The other person does whatever he or she is told to do.

The part the movies don't get across is how scared that second person is. I wanted to cry. I wanted to run. I wanted to sob, but I did what he ordered me to do.

"Turn around."

He pushed me farther into darkness, toward the back wall.

"Open it!"

I was bewildered. There was no door. Horizontal boards, in perfect rows, started at the floor and ended at the ceiling. Knotholes punctuated the boards here and there.

"Open it!"

He reached around me and slipped two fingers into a pair of holes. He lifted the back panel, and it shifted slightly. Then he stepped back and motioned with the gun.

"Open it!"

I dropped my flashlight and heard it clatter away. Fumbling with my right hand, I found the two holes he had used and, with my left, discovered two others. It took surprisingly little effort to lift the panel and slip it off its supports. I slid it behind the end of the shelves on my left. I was looking into a dark cavern.

Mr. Pitt watched me. He was trembling, but the hand with the gun never shook at all.

"Hurry," he growled.

It felt as if I was going into another world, a world filled with darkness and the heavy odor of damp soil. I was suddenly cold, but I couldn't tell whether the cold was coming from the chamber before me, or from within. I stepped forward into a dark cell carved out of the earth.

The only light came from my flashlight, which lay behind me on the cellar floor. The beam cast crazy shadows, but I could make out the general shape of the hidden chamber. Hard packed dirt formed a level floor that ran back into blackness. Two massive wood beams on each side supported cross beams overhead. Stretched over the cross beams was a makeshift wooden ceiling. When I looked up, a drop of cold water fell from the ceiling onto my forehead.

The dark earth absorbed light like a sponge, so the whole room was a mosaic of shadow and deeper shadow. The walls were rough and craggy, and they slanted toward each other. The wall on my right was all packed rock and dirt, as if it had been filled with rubble from one of the old mines. Near it was a pile of loose earth and rock. Someone had been digging.

I squinted, trying to make out the farthest corner. What looked like a large bundle of rags scuttled backwards and stopped against the far wall.

Mr. Pitt shoved me forward into the darkness. I heard a click, and the chamber filled with light.

The bundle straightened. I realized this must be the thing I had heard bumping against the wall. This pitiful creature had frightened me terribly, before I knew what I truly had to fear, and before I knew what fear truly was.

Eyes, filled with terror, flashed from behind long, straggly black hair. I recognized the form as human, thankfully washing away the horrid beast of my imagination.

Well, I had solved one part of the mystery. I had found Susan.

Her bare arms glistened with the dampness seeping from the ceiling. She had burrowed into a pile of burlap bags and dirty canvas, but clearly she was cold, and wet, and very frightened.

"Put it back," Mr. Pitt said, indicating the wall panel. He held a large electric lantern in one hand and gestured with the gun he held in the other.

From the inside it was easy to see how the false wall was designed. Huge metal hooks hung from the upright beams and held it. I slipped the wall hangers over the hooks, and the panel settled into place. My flashlight had come to rest against a basket of apples. As I worked I watched its glow fade, flicker, and die. Part of my hope died with it.

Mr. Pitt grabbed me roughly from behind and shoved me to the back of the cell. My elbow hit the stone wall, and a sharp pain screeched up my arm. Tears flooded my eyes, and I cried out.

"Shut up!" he shouted.

I stumbled over Susan and fell in a heap beside her. A pile of junk lay between us. Mr. Pitt grabbed some rope and filthy rags from the pile. He pulled my hands behind me, and pain wrenched my elbow again. When I whimpered, he pulled the rope tighter and smiled. I promised myself not to let him know if he hurt me again. I wouldn't give him the satisfaction.

He stuffed the disgusting rags into my mouth. It hurt when he tied clothesline around my head to hold the gag in place, but this time I refused to cry.

He pushed me back against the wall and tied my ankles. I sat there, helpless, beside Susan, feeling like the world's foremost defective detective. I had planned to fix everything for everyone and had wound up here. All I could do was concentrate on breathing and try to keep my weight off my aching arm.

Mr. Pitt whistled softly under his breath. With a shiver of revulsion, I recognized the tune GrandAnn had been humming the night before. Mr. Pitt,

117

without even a glance in our direction, picked up his electric lantern and a pick and moved to the back edge of the rock wall.

Tap. Tap. Tap.

It was an innocent little sound. It wasn't frightening at all, by itself. It brought back, though, the terror I had felt last week when I came for the apples. It was a sinister sound after all.

Tap. Tap. Tap.

His pick struck the rocky wall. But why? I was entirely mystified. Had he lost his mind? Was he searching for buried treasure? For gold?

Gold. The back-yard miners dug for dust, but the gold-bearing earth had to be washed through huge sluice boxes. He certainly wasn't mining. He was just digging.

I couldn't know how many hours had gone by, but my stomach was sure it was past dinner time. I was stiff and cold, and the damp earth above dripped endlessly.

Susan's eyes had long since closed. Her breathing was regular. I thought she must be asleep, although I couldn't imagine sleeping in that musty cold. Then I realized that she might have been tied up there for days. She was lucky even to be alive.

Mr. Pitt kept tapping at the stone, gradually digging out chunks. Sometimes he used a small shovel to move the earth. I concentrated on what he was doing, mystified, frightened, and fascinated.

Here was a riddle worth solving.

Now and then he would take out a tape measure

118

and use a piece of chalk to mark the wall. He never stopped to rest. He never glanced at us. The only sound was his quiet whistling, and the tap, tap, tap of his pick.

"Miranda!"

Faint and distant, GrandAnn's voice penetrated through the root cellar wall. It grew louder. The outer door opened and her steps sounded on the root cellar floor.

"Miranda!"

My heart raced.

Chapter 18

Mr. Pitt's head jerked up. He grabbed his gun and pushed it into the back of my head, painfully. I didn't dare make a sound. I wasn't just afraid for myself. He might hurt GrandAnn. Still, my heart was wrenched as I heard her footsteps retreat and the door slam.

I think we all held our breath until the silence flowed around us like rising water. Finally Mr. Pitt stepped away and turned back to his relentless tapping. He didn't seem to notice the passing hours.

"Yes, yes, here it is," he said at last, and the tapping stopped.

He had dislodged a large rock from the wall. In the gap left by the rock I could dimly make out a metallic glitter.

He strained to lift a tin box from the hollow in the stone. He sat on the floor next to the light and brushed dirt tenderly from his prize. I heard his keys clatter as he selected one and worked it into the opening on the box. He struggled to twist the key.

The lid squealed as the old hinges finally budged open, and Mr. Pitt echoed the sound. His face was

120

covered with sweat, and it shone as he gazed down. He lifted a leather pouch out of the strongbox, untied the thong binding it, and poured something into his open palm. The lantern's light revealed a pile of fine dust and grit that glowed with a soft luster. Gold!

He saw me staring and he looked almost surprised, as though he had forgotten Susan and me. He grinned at us, but I wished he hadn't. His grin was more frightening than his scowl.

Replacing the gold dust with gentle care, he wiped the box with an old rag. A name was spelled out in white letters on the side. The name was Al Minor.

He traced the letters with a dirty finger. "That's me. Did you catch on? I couldn't resist the hint, the Concerto in *A Minor*. It was just a bit of a game I played. Just one more secret."

He held the metal box close to his chest, close to his heart, as if it were someone he loved. He closed his eyes and was silent for a moment. His voice grew stronger as he told his story.

"Fifty years ago," he whispered, "I was older than you are by just a few years. I was fifteen. Your grandmother was still a baby. She would come to visit with her folks, but in those days her grandparents lived here. Her grandfather hired me to help out around the place. I worked hard, but it was hard times. Everyone struggled, but no one got ahead.

"He was doing a little mining here in the back, like almost everyone else. It didn't pay much. I don't

121

think he ever suspected that the reason it didn't pay better was because I was taking just a bit of the gold dust out of each day's gleanings.

"He was a fool. I think it must run in your family. He just left the dust in a leather pouch on the kitchen table. He trusted everyone. Like I said, he was a fool.

"Well, I stashed the stolen dust in this same tin box. I didn't have anywhere really safe to keep it, so I cut a hidey hole into the rock here. I covered it with a big rock, and I was always around, so I could move it if the digging started in that direction. Besides, it had my name on it. Ann's grandfather would never have looked inside. He would have figured it was my property.

"There was this other operation down the street, just about where that cave-in happened. It was a big project, run by a pair of rough guys. Their sluice boxes ran all day, from before dawn to after dark.

"One Friday night they finished late. One of the fellows wanted to quit early and take the week's haul to the bank, but the other wanted to run one last load. It turned out they worked past the bank's closing time, so they lugged the gold home with them.

"I used to hang around, in case anything fell my way. I overheard them talking that night and followed them. I was careful to stay well back. It wouldn't do to have them think I was after anything of theirs. I wasn't, anyway. I just had this curiosity about where they were going to stash all that gold.

"Well, wouldn't you know, they started to argue. The little one was mad that they'd missed the bank hours and the big one, named Ned, said the little guy was lazy. It started like that but it got a whole lot more personal. Finally they decided to have it out right there.

"I was watching from behind a lilac hedge, more scared than ever that they would see me. I didn't even dare run, because they would know I had been following them.

"Ned, he was mean as poison oak in July. He grabbed a board and hit his partner over the head. The little guy was about done for. He lay on the ground and Ned knelt over him, still shouting mad. While he was concentrating on his partner, I saw my chance. I grabbed their gold and ran.

"I nearly got away, too, but Ned looked up just in time to see me. He shouted after me, called me by name. Al. They didn't call me by my full name in those days.

"When I heard he had recognized me, I ran even harder. I got here, put the box in my hidey hole, and went in to supper.

"Ned came for me that night. He tapped on my window and called me out. I was plain scared. I stayed right there, where he couldn't get to me, but before dawn I sneaked out the back door. I'd have stopped for the gold, but Ann's grandfather was already digging in here. I just left.

"I heard later that Ned's partner died so he was in a heap more trouble than I was. I changed my name and moved around a lot, drifting from place to place. I came back once, thinking to collect my stake of gold dust, but the old mine was mostly filled in. I never had a chance to dig around. I wound up going east, played in bands, and went on with life, but I never forgot.

"When your grandmother took over the inn, I realized my box might still be within reach. She didn't know about this secret mine, but I had heard her granddad planning it. He claimed there was more gold in the canned apricots than in the ground, but he couldn't resist leaving a bit of the old mine here.

"I decided to take a chance and move in. Ann didn't know me. Neither did that old bat Prescott. They were too involved with their own selves to care anyway.

"All these years I've been waiting for my due. All these years."

His eyes focused on us and hardened. Susan's shoulders shook. Her muffled sobs unnerved me. I had been so caught up in Mr. Pitt's story that, for a moment, I didn't think of the danger we were in.

"This little girl has given me a bonus. Like a bonus for my long wait. She brought me these letters. I guess they're worth a lot of money, too."

He opened the violin case wide and showed me the letters nestled there. He slipped his gun into the case and latched it.

"You and your folks kept me away from my

fortune all these years. Now I'll leave you here in place. It's kind of like one of those riddles your twice-great-grandfather used to like so much. When is buried treasure not buried treasure? Why, when it's your own granddaughter."

He smirked horribly as he locked his tin box again. He dragged it and his violin case to the doorway, lifted the false wall aside, and backed through. In growing despair, I watched him pull the box and case onto the floor of the root cellar. Hope shivered through me when I realized he couldn't carry the lantern as well as his violin case and the heavy box. At least we would have the light.

My hope shriveled into helplessness when he gave me a savage smile, then reached in and switched off the electric lantern.

Darkness filled the chamber. I heard the wall sliding back into place and Mr. Pitt's footsteps on the stairs. The door to the shed closed with a single thud, and the padlock grated into place.

Chapter 19

The last sounds faded, and my world collapsed to hold only two things: Susan's muted cries, and darkness. Usually darkness is just an absence of light, but this was so real, so solid, that I thought I could actually touch it. It filled every niche and rough corner of the little den where Susan and I were imprisoned.

Susan continued to cry. Her desperate fear rolled off of her and engulfed me. I wanted to shake her. I wanted to cry, too.

I tried to concentrate. It must have been past midnight. GrandAnn had been looking for me, but she had checked the shed and thought I wasn't there. It might be a long time before she came back. It was up to me, again. I just hoped I would do a better job this time. My idea of solving the mystery wrapped in a riddle had backfired. Actually, it had exploded in my face, more like a mystery wrapped in a firecracker.

Blackness was everywhere, so it didn't matter if my eyes were open or closed, but I closed them and tried to imagine every detail of the shed. Unfortunately, one of my first images was of cobwebs, and that made me think of spiders.

Spiders the size of basketballs, I thought, and mice, and moles, and rats.

Rats! Ugh! I tried to think about something else. I thought crazily about how Dad liked to joke that Noah lit the ark with *flood*lights. That's what I needed, but I would settle for a candle, or even a lightning bug.

"Concentrate," I told myself and went back to visualizing our prison. I remembered Mr. Pitt backing out of the hidden mine and reaching to switch off the lantern. I could still see it in my imagination, just inside the entrance. Maybe I could find it, even in the sooty dark.

It was impossible to orient myself in the total blackness, but I thought I was facing the right direction. I scooted forward but moved too fast. With my hands bound, my balance was off, and I fell heavily on my right side.

Thankful I hadn't fallen on my injured arm, I inched forward like a caterpillar toward the lantern. At least the rushing sound of my breathing drowned out Susan's sobs.

With all of my attention focused on finding the light, I wasn't really aware of the other creature there in the darkness with us. Not really aware . . . but . . . yes, there it was again, a soft presence behind me.

Something warm brushed against the back of my neck, something warm and hairy.

I wanted to scream, but I couldn't force a sound through the rags in my mouth. I wanted to scream even more than I wanted to get out of there. I wanted to scream and cry and shout and run and shriek. Instead, I started to shake, all at once, all over.

It swept across my face now. Then it returned and brushed across my face again and down my back, to my imprisoned hands. It rubbed against my hands.

"Meow."

Orenthal must have come in with GrandAnn and sneaked into the mine in the darkness while Mr. Pitt wrestled with the false wall. If he had said hello to Susan, her frantic cries made even more sense.

I'm afraid that thought cheered me up. I guess I'll never be as full of goodwill as GrandAnn.

I wiggled my fingers and was rewarded with a hearty purr. Orenthal twisted his head against my hands, and I felt calm returning. My mind cleared, and I began to form a plan.

First, light. I squirmed across the rough dirt floor with new energy. A last mighty thrust brought my head firmly against the lantern. I heard it fall. I rolled over to bring my hands against it. Fumbling, I found the switch and, even though the angle was awkward, I urged it up.

The chamber filled with light.

Susan's sobs stopped. Orenthal sat in front of her, watching her with a serious expression. I would have smiled if I had been able to move my mouth.

Susan certainly didn't smile. She twisted around

128

and kicked at him. He backed off a bit and continued to regard her.

Some people hate cats. It's that simple.

My head and hands and arms and legs all hurt, especially my left elbow, but my heart didn't hurt anymore. The light and Orenthal's persistent self-assurance gave me all the confidence I needed.

Now to get rid of the rope. I thought of breaking the lantern to use a sharp edge, but I couldn't face the darkness again. Then I saw the shovel Mr. Pitt had used. The digging edge might be sharp enough to cut the rope.

I struggled to the shovel and sawed the rope across it. Each stroke sent electric jolts of pain through my left arm. Sweat broke out on my face, and I was warm for the first time in hours. Susan watched and shivered. She had stopped crying, but I almost preferred her noise to this new silence.

Finally the rope gave way. I worked with stiff fingers to free myself of that awful gag. My mouth tasted like cotton balls dipped in dirt.

Then I gave Orenthal an enormous hug. He blinked in appreciation and purred louder.

It was Susan's turn. Orenthal and I looked at her for just a moment while I considered what I should do. I still wanted to shout at her about stealing GrandAnn's letters, but she looked so miserable I didn't have the heart to do it. Instead I untied the bundle of rags around her mouth.

She sucked in huge gulps of air and licked her

lips. I knew how she felt. My own mouth was painfully dry, and my jaws felt broken. I had only been gagged for a couple of hours.

"How long have you been here, Susan?"

"I don't know. Since Sunday night," she whispered hoarsely. "Water, please, I need water."

I had heard that people can survive without food for a long time, but they quickly die without water. That was when I fully realized that Mr. Pitt really didn't care if we died in there.

"Just a second. I'll be right back."

I tugged the door out of its brackets and broke free into the shed. Compared to the musty prison behind me, the root cellar felt open and airy, even friendly. I was so glad to be free I would have been pleased to shake hands with a spider, even one the size of a basketball.

I grabbed a jar of apricots and pried the lid off against the edge of the shelf. I wanted to sip the sweet syrup myself, but took it to Susan and held it against her lips.

When she had swallowed about half the syrup, I untied her wrists and ankles. She was still shivering uncontrollably, so I pulled off my jacket and heavy sweater and covered her. Orenthal crowded close with his soft warmth.

Susan smiled at me then, and whispered, "Thanks, Miranda."

I don't know what happened to me. Maybe it was being so scared. Maybe it was GrandAnn's attitude about "the benefit of a doubt." I remembered

Georgette saying that stuck-up people were sometimes just shy. Whatever the reason, I hugged Susan, hard, with my right arm. She hugged me back. We cried together, and I learned you can't cry and hug and hate all at once.

I left Susan with Orenthal. She worked on the rest of the juice and the apricots while I returned for two more jars, one for each of us. When I came back I saw something I will never forget.

I guess GrandAnn is right when she says anyone can change. We just need to give them the chance, and a little kindness.

Susan was holding an apricot out to Orenthal. His tail drew little circles high in the air as he ran his tongue over the sweet fruit.

Chapter 20

I stood on the top step beside Susan. We banged on the door with our shoes and shouted. Susan's voice was still not strong but I made up for her.

"Help! GrandAnn, help!"

It must have been after midnight. I was sure they would be looking for me. The problem was that they wouldn't be looking for Mr. Pitt, and he had the letters.

I pounded harder and shouted louder.

"Help! In here! Help!"

Orenthal retreated back into the mine to get away from the undignified commotion.

Suddenly the door popped open. We had been making so much noise we hadn't heard GrandAnn calling out.

"Thunder," she said, and she swept me into her warm arms. "How did you two get locked in the root cellar?"

The question sounded at once so reasonable, and so absurd, that I almost laughed aloud.

After a trip to the emergency room, where my arm was x-rayed and I was given a sling, but, thank goodness, not a cast, we sat together in the comfort of the Becky Thatcher Room. Dawn filled the room with warmth.

Mrs. Prescott and Officer Carlson had arrived. Nick and Julie had fixed breakfast and hot spiced cider made from GrandAnn's apples. Susan and I nestled on the soft couch, with GrandAnn between us.

"It was your friends who first put us on to Al Pitt," GrandAnn began. "When I found your note but couldn't find you, I called Georgette. She suggested I talk to Tiff and Jess. They explained about Tiff's photograph and how the violin had been playing at the same time that Mr. Pitt was in the shed.

"The hint in your note sent me out there, but all I found was a mess on the floor and the lightning bug flashlight. That scared me. I called Officer Carlson, and while I waited for him, I went up to the attic and looked in the secret hiding place. Sure enough, your journal was there."

She tightened her arm around my shoulder, being careful not to put pressure on my elbow. I squirmed closer, appreciating the warmth even more after the dark and damp of my night's adventure.

"You had it figured out, Miranda, except for the part about the old mine. Thunder, even I didn't know about that! I showed your journal to the officer, and he agreed that he should ask Mr. Pitt some questions. When we realized he was gone, too, the police started to look for him."

Officer Carlson spoke up. "Well, we got him. You gave us such good information that we were after him before he actually left."

At least I had helped a little. The way he talked, I had helped a lot. So had Georgette, Tiff, and Jess. We were a team.

GrandAnn agreed. "Without Miranda and her friends, we would have let Mr. Pitt get away with the letters, the gold, and" — she hugged Susan — "murder!"

"He had just barely gotten to the freeway when we spotted him," the officer continued. "He was mad as a cat in a rainstorm when we took these from him."

He handed GrandAnn the packet of letters. She tenderly opened the first one.

"Dear Anne," she read, "I feel a great need to forward my thanks for your generous hospitality and that of your parents. Thunder, it's been a long time since these poor teeth encountered biscuits such as yours, and my tongue is in a melting mood at the memory.

"Life and travel have continued exciting since my stop with you in Yreka."

She settled back on the couch and took Susan's hand in hers. "So this half of the riddle is solved. The letters are back where they belong. Susan has told me a little bit about why she took them, and I think she should tell the rest of you."

"I guess I owe you all an apology," Susan said. "I didn't realize I could be getting you into trouble,

Nick. And I didn't really think Julie could be arrested just because the letters were in her room.

"Mostly, I was just thinking about myself. When Ann found the letters, I was almost as excited as she was. I thought I might be able to use them for a special project at the college.

"I was looking at the picture in the attic and thinking it wasn't fair that I couldn't have it in my room when I found the envelope taped to the back. I took the letters.

"I was just going to make copies to use in my project. I thought it would help me get a teaching job next year. I never intended to keep the originals, but after I copied the first one, I realized I could substitute it for the real letter, and Ann would probably never even notice."

She ducked her head, but GrandAnn squeezed her hand gently and whispered, "Go on."

"Well, I replaced the first letter right away, before Ann sent it to San Francisco. Then I worked on copies of the others. I had finished, and I was still thinking I should keep the copies and return the real letters, but then Ann found out they were missing, and it was too late. I convinced myself that I wasn't doing any real harm, but really, Ann, I knew it was wrong."

She lifted her head and stared bravely at Officer Carlson.

"I'm ready to take my punishment, but I'm so glad you caught that miserable man. He told me he knew about my forgery and promised me if I met

135

him and gave him the letters, he would see that Ann got them back. I was just going to give them to him and leave town. I was so ashamed.

"When I met him in the root cellar last Sunday evening, he took the letters and laughed at me. He stuck me in that awful den, in the dark. He didn't even give me water.

"Miranda saved my life. Miranda and Orenthal tried to comfort me, when I had been hateful to them both. I'll never be able to repay their kindness," she said, "nor yours, Ann. I don't know how you can forgive me, but I want you to know I'm sorry."

She bent over to scratch Orenthal behind his ears. Nick and Julie stared as Orenthal jumped into Susan's lap.

"No forgiveness is necessary," GrandAnn said. "And we'll find a way for you to use the letters in your studies, too. After all, Mark Twain belongs to the whole world."

"It's up to Ann to decide what should be done about the letters," Officer Carlson said sternly. Then his expression softened, and he added, "Somehow, I don't think she will want to testify against you, Susan."

"Not if she treats Susan the way she has treated Nick," Julie said with a grateful tone.

I wasn't really surprised to notice that Nick was sitting on the arm of the big chair with Julie curled up on the seat, smiling at him. They were holding hands.

Mrs. Prescott beamed at them. "Kindness runs in Ann's family," she said. "In fact, that's how a lot of this trouble started. Ann's grandfather took in a poor orphaned boy and trusted him. He turned out to be a rascal."

"Mr. Pitt, you mean?" I asked, thinking I would have used a stronger word than *rascal.*

"Yes. He's the one who knocked me out that day. It started to come back to me when your friends told Ann that he was in the shed and in his room at the same time. I gradually remembered more.

"I had gone into his room to clean that afternoon. I thought he was there because I could hear his violin. When he didn't answer my knock, I thought something was wrong, so I opened the door. Imagine my surprise when I found the music was coming from his tape recorder.

"He came in while I was standing there. He shouted at me and followed me down the hall, and that must have been when he hit me with the Mark Twain bust.

"The more I remembered, the more I was sure I had known him before. Then Miranda made that remark about the Concerto in A Minor. Maybe he meant it as some kind of sly joke. Anyway, it was his real name.

"Back in the Depression, I knew him as Al, Al Minor. He was school age but he didn't go to school. He worked for Ann's grandfather, and I used to see him around. Sometimes he helped my folks out, too. I had kind of a crush on him."

I tried to imagine Mr. Pitt . . . Minor . . . as a young boy, with Mrs. Prescott mooning over him, but I was too tired to stretch my imagination that hard.

"Then he disappeared one night," she continued. "We were all afraid something terrible had happened to him."

"I guess it had," GrandAnn said. "And it made him bitter and mad at the world."

"He'll have even more reason to be mad now," Officer Carlson added. "We're charging him with embezzlement, theft, assault, kidnapping, and even attempted murder. He'll have a lot to think about."

I didn't go to school on Wednesday. GrandAnn and Mrs. Prescott fussed over Susan and me all day. It felt good to be pampered.

On Thursday morning Georgette and I arrived at the library to find Jess and Tiff already there, along with Tim, Josh, and Steve.

They had made a big paper badge that said OF-FICIAL HERO, and Tiff giggled while she pinned it on my sweater. Then she made me stand against the check-out desk and hold a stack of Mark Twain books, while she took my picture.

"For the school paper," she explained unnecessarily.

They made me repeat over and over the story of how I was trapped in the hidden mine. Jess took notes. Georgette gasped and shuddered at the scary

138

parts. Josh wanted to know who the gold belonged to now.

"The police officer said it would go to the heirs of the people Mr. Pitt stole it from," I told him. "That probably means mostly to GrandAnn."

Tim asked if he could come over and see the old mine sometime, and we all agreed to go together after school. At least all but Steve.

"Come on," I said, feeling bold now that I was an official hero. "We'd like to have you. GrandAnn will fix hot chocolate."

He nodded, then muttered, "Thanks."

Georgette said later that she thinks he is just shy.

I told her everyone is a little lonely and a little shy. That's what friends are for.

Afterword

When Mark Twain was a young man, he worked as a newspaper reporter and traveled in the gold country of northern California. We know he was in the area of Yreka, California, and the story of how Yreka got its name is based on one of his newspaper reports.

Mark Twain enjoyed a good riddle or joke. He was interested in doubles of all kinds, including twins and double meanings, such as puns. That is one reason he chose Twain as his pen name. His given name was Samuel Clemens.

The back-yard mines of the Great Depression years are a historic fact. Maps are available of some of the mining sites, but there are many others that have been forgotten. We hope they have all been filled in, but now and then streets in southern Oregon still collapse because of undermining in years past.

The phrase "wrapped in a riddle" came out of a comment made by former British Prime Minister Winston Churchill about the complex and secretive society of Soviet Russia. He said it was a "riddle wrapped in a mystery enmeshed in an enigma." That phrase suggested the title of this book, and even some parts of the story.